THE MADMAN OF
BLACK BEAR MOUNTAIN

READ ALL THE MYSTERIES IN THE
HARDY BOYS ADVENTURES:

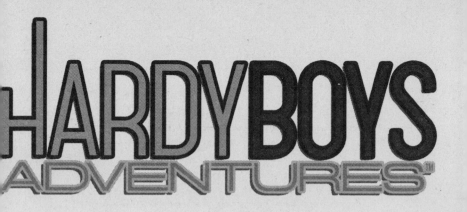

#12 *THE MADMAN OF BLACK BEAR MOUNTAIN*

FRANKLIN W. DIXON

ALADDIN   New York London Toronto Sydney New Delhi

ALADDIN

An imprint of Simon & Schuster Children's Publishing Division
1230 Avenue of the Americas, New York, NY 10020
This Aladdin paperback edition June 2016
Text copyright © 2016 by Simon & Schuster, Inc.
Cover illustration copyright © 2016 by Kevin Keele
Also available in an Aladdin hardcover edition.
All rights reserved, including the right of reproduction in whole or in part in any form.
ALADDIN is a trademark of Simon & Schuster, Inc.,
and related logo is a registered trademark of Simon & Schuster, Inc.
THE HARDY BOYS MYSTERY STORIES, HARDY BOYS ADVENTURES,
and related logo are trademarks of Simon & Schuster, Inc.
For information about special discounts for bulk purchases, please contact
Simon & Schuster Special Sales at 1-866-506-1949 or business@simonandschuster.com.
The Simon & Schuster Speakers Bureau can bring authors to your live event.
For more information or to book an event contact the Simon & Schuster Speakers Bureau
at 1-866-248-3049 or visit our website at www.simonspeakers.com.
Cover designed by Karin Paprocki
Interior designed by Mike Rosamilia
The text of this book was set in Adobe Caslon Pro.
Manufactured in the United States of America 0516 OFF
10 9 8 7 6 5 4 3 2 1
Library of Congress Control Number 2016932670
ISBN 978-1-4814-3881-0 (hc)
ISBN 978-1-4814-3880-3 (pbk)
ISBN 978-1-4814-3882-7 (eBook)

CONTENTS

THE MADMAN OF BLACK BEAR MOUNTAIN

ZIP IT! 1

JOE

I COULD STILL HEAR MY BROTHER'S SCREAMS echoing across the river valley as a woman with a bear-paw tattoo shoved me off the ledge and sent me hurtling after him.

And it was awesome!

My body rocketed through the atmosphere at fifty miles per hour, with the wind punching me in the face so hard, my eyes watered. Just when it seemed like I might plummet to my death, I started zipping straight ahead, my feet gliding over the treetops like I was surfing on air. Only this wasn't a dream or a video game. It was spring break!

The zip line shot me over a lush mountain valley toward the rustic lodge just across the river where Frank and the rest of the Bayport High Green Environment Conservation

Club (GECC, or, as we liked to call ourselves, the Geccos) were getting ready for our camping expedition to a nearby scientific research station. From my bird's-eye view, I could see all the way upstream past a thundering waterfall and miles of rolling hills to our destination atop the tallest, most forbidding peak, Black Bear Mountain.

"Yee-haw!" I hollered as I zipped over the river toward the landing platform.

Normally, I wouldn't get this excited about spending spring break on a school trip with one of Frank's nerdy clubs, but most nerdy school trips don't involve staying someplace as cool as Bear Foot Lodge for part of it. They also don't usually include a pair of girls as cute as "the Ms," which was what everyone called BFFs Mandy and Melissa. I'd been trying to catch Mandy's eye, and I know Melissa had already caught Frank's.

I'd talked him into doing the zip line to impress her, but judging from how loudly he'd screamed and how pale he was when I reached the bottom, I think my plan may have backfired.

"Why did I let you talk me into that?" he asked as I unhooked myself from the zip line's harness.

"Because we're Hardys," I replied. "And Hardys never back down from a challenge."

"Chasing bad guys and solving crimes is one thing," he said, referring to our sideline as Bayport's foremost teenage detectives. "Voluntarily jumping off a cliff is another."

"I'm with you, Frank," Mandy said, brushing back her long auburn hair. "I'm ready to leave all this daredevil stuff behind and check out Dr. Kroopnik's research station."

"That's because you guys are a couple of total nerds," Melissa said, playfully pushing her best friend.

Oh no! It looked like Frank and I had crushes on the wrong Ms!

"Right!?" I agreed with Melissa. "I don't know which was better, that zip line or the white-water rafting we did this morning. And we haven't even gotten a chance to go horse-back riding yet."

We'd arrived at Bear Foot Lodge the previous afternoon, and today we were scheduled to head up to Black Bear Mountain. While helping noted biologist Dr. Kroopnik with his field research for a few days, we'd be camping out in the woods.

"It was really cool of your parents to arrange for us to stay here, Randall," Melissa said to the fifth and final member of the Geccos. "This place is awesome."

"Yeah, I guess," Randall grumbled as he tried to brush dirt off his no-longer-perfectly-white Converse All Stars. "If you like bugs and country bumpkins."

Randall must have ignored the part about us roughing it in the woods, because he was still wearing his standard prep-ster combo of brand-new sneakers and a cardigan draped over his shoulders. With his attitude, he should have just worn a wet blanket instead.

"Are you kidding, dude?" I asked. "If our parents took us here every year, I'd be totally stoked."

"Yeah, Randall, you're just grumpy because we voted Frank club president instead of you," Mandy said.

"Like I even care about this stupid club," he scoffed. "I'm only here because my parents think this Kroopnik guy's name will look good on my college applications."

"Who's ready for some science!" GECC faculty adviser Jim shouted through an armload of camping gear as he stumbled toward us. He seemed to be carrying more stuff than he could handle.

Frank and Mandy whooped it up.

"Assisting Dr. Kroopnik with his field research is going to be a great experience for you guys. I—Ayeeee!" Jim tripped over his feet before he could finish, sending both him and the gear flying.

Bayport High's fresh-out-of-college science teacher chuckled as Frank and I ran over to help him up. "Sorry about that, guys. I probably should have asked for help, but I'm just so excited to get this adventure started that I couldn't wait."

That was Jim Morgan in a nutshell, full of more enthusiasm than grace. Jim—who insisted students call him by his first name—had been at Bayport High for only a couple of semesters, but he was already one of the students' favorite teachers—partly because he was a great teacher and partly because he was endlessly entertaining. You never knew when he might accidentally set the chem lab on fire or walk into a wall absentmindedly while pondering an exciting new lesson plan.

"Max Kroopnik is a real-deal field biologist," he said, readjusting his glasses. "The man has had studies published in just about every major science journal there is."

"His article on the effects of carbon emissions on endangered species in high-elevation river ecosystems has led to a whole new way of thinking about mountain preservation," Frank eagerly added.

"Totally," Mandy chimed in. "I can't wait to see his new method for on-site stream water filtration."

Melissa and I caught each other rolling our eyes at the same time and laughed.

"Incoming!" a woman's voice called out as Casey, one half of the young couple who owned Bear Foot Lodge, whooshed toward us on the zip line.

"You guys did great up there," she said, unhooking herself from the zip line and hopping off the platform.

"Your tattoo is wicked, Casey." Melissa pointed at the bear paw on Casey's forearm below the rolled-up sleeve of her red plaid lumberjack shirt. Not that Casey looked like a lumberjack. With her long blond hair, bright smile, and trendy sunglasses, she looked more like an outdoor clothing catalog model.

"Cool, right?" Casey said, tracing the squiggly line running through the center of the bear paw. "It's kind of like my family crest. My sister has one too. That line follows the same path as the river through this valley."

"And before anyone even asks," Jim interjected, "no, you are not allowed to get tattoos on this trip."

Casey laughed. "We should go ahead and get your gear loaded on the plane. The pilot will be here soon to fly you up to Black Bear Mountain so you can rendezvous with the scientist."

Jim looked apprehensively at the small single-propeller bush plane waiting in the field next to the lodge. "There's no way we can take an off-road vehicle or just hike in?"

"Sorry. Black Bear Mountain is about as remote as it gets around here, and the research station is in an old ranger lookout post near the very top." Casey pointed toward the peak looming over the rest of the valley in the distance. "There are no roads, and you'd have to be an experienced mountaineer to make it to the trailhead on foot."

"I'm game," I said, thinking about how cool it would be to put my mountain-climbing skills to the test.

"I don't doubt it, Joe." Casey gave me an approving nod. "But I'm not so sure about the rest of your group. If you guys don't want to fly, there are plenty of great places to camp right around here that are more accessible."

"But what about Dr. Kroopnik?" Frank protested.

"It's okay, Frank," Jim said resolutely. "I'm not going to let my silly little phobia about flying spoil our expedition." He took a deep breath and turned to Casey. "It's just a short flight, right?"

"Just about the shortest you'll ever take," she replied. "You'll be back on the ground in a few minutes."

Jim gulped. "Okay, we might as well get on with—"

Jim was interrupted by a bang so loud, it sounded like a gunshot. We turned to see a beat-up old boat of a red convertible backfiring as it squealed around the corner and swerved up the drive toward the lodge at top speed. The driver slammed on the brakes at the last second, plowing through a pair of trash cans before coming to a stop a few feet from the porch.

The guy who stumbled out had on big green-tinted aviator glasses and quite possibly the brightest, ugliest Hawaiian shirt I'd ever seen. He took off his floppy hat, scratched his shiny bald dome, and let out a loud belch that we could hear all the way across the field.

"Um, who's that?" Jim asked Casey.

"The Commander," she replied. "Your pilot."

FRIGHT FLIGHT

2

FRANK

"ARE YOU CRAZY?!" JIM YANKED ON his hair with both hands as he looked from our so-called pilot to Casey and back again. "He can't even park a car without crashing, how's he supposed to land an airplane on top of a mountain?"

The wacky-looking guy in the blinding shirt had gone from belching to hopping up and down on one leg and hitting himself on the side of the head like he was trying to shake water out of his ears. I may not have shared our teacher's fear of flying, but I was asking myself the same question.

"Trust me, Commander Gonzo may not look it," Casey said, "but he's the best bush pilot in the state."

"Commander Gonzo?! What kind of name is Gonzo?" Jim groaned. "He sounds like a Muppet, not a pilot!"

Casey's husband, Steven, loped toward us from the lodge. Tall and skinny, with a lumberjack shirt like Casey's, a rugged yet well-maintained beard, and stylish retro black-framed glasses, he looked like a cross between a cool hipster and a young mountain man.

"Hey, is something wrong, guys?" he asked, scrunching his brow.

Casey said, "Jim is just a little nervous about the flight to Black Bear Mountain with the Commander."

We watched as said Commander began rooting through his car's trunk, tossing a variety of junk over his shoulders as he went.

"Anybody seen my spare parachute?" he shouted to Marty, Bear Foot Lodge's burly fishing guide, who had come outside after Steven to see what all the commotion was about.

Steven nervously cleared his throat as he looked from Commander Gonzo back to Jim. "Uh, yeah, I can see how you might feel that way. Maybe you should just skip the flight to Black Bear Mountain and camp at one of our great spots around here instead."

Jim was starting to worry me. From the way he was gnawing on a fingernail, he looked like he was giving the suggestion serious thought.

"But what about meeting Dr. Kroopnik?" I asked.

"Yeah!" Mandy and Randall chimed in.

9

"I suggested the same thing," Casey told Steven, "but they don't want to miss out on their research trip."

Steven tugged on his beard and stared off into the distance at Black Bear Mountain like he was trying to solve a difficult puzzle.

"Hey, tell you what," he said after a minute. "We've got a buddy who's a wildlife ranger right here in the valley. I bet he'd be happy to have you guys tag along for a day or two. It would be just as educational as some stuffy scientist and a lot more exciting, but without all the hassle! What do you say? I'll get on the radio and let him know you're coming."

Steven gestured back at the lodge, where they kept their two-way ham radio. We were far enough up in the mountains that there wasn't any cell phone service, so sometimes the only way to reach people deep in the backcountry was still by radio. Jim had never even talked to Dr. Kroopnik; they'd coordinated the whole trip by sending letters, like in the old days!

The rest of the Geccos and I looked anxiously at our teacher. I don't think any of us were thrilled about getting on a plane with Commander Gonzo, but we didn't want to miss out on the trip to Black Bear Mountain, either.

"No, we've already gone to a lot of trouble to make arrangements with Dr. Kroopnik," Jim finally declared. "He's expecting us, and I don't want to let him or my students down."

"Are you sure?" Steven frowned. "That far up Black Bear Mountain is practically the middle of nowhere. Once you get out there, you're stuck for three whole nights until

Gonzo comes back for you. And the weather at that elevation can turn on you real quick. It can be rough camping if you're not used to it."

He eyed Randall, who'd been busy trying to defend his cardigan from bugs.

"I'll be fine, thanks," Randall said sarcastically. "Putting Kroopnik's name on my college applications is the only reason I let my parents talk me into coming back to this place."

"You sure?" Steven insisted. "You don't usually go in for all the outdoorsy stuff when your family comes up."

"You're right, we could always just call the trip off, and then I could just tell my parents to cancel their check." Randall fixed Steven with a chilly glare. "I mean, it's not like you guys need the money or anything, right?"

"Randall!" Jim snapped.

"What?" Randall asked fake innocently.

"Nobody is canceling anything," Jim sighed. "We came here to see Dr. Kroopnik and we're going to see Dr. Kroopnik. If Casey says it's safe to fly with this Gonzo guy, I believe her."

Steven was about to say something else when Casey placed her hand gently on his shoulder. "Come on, honey," she said. "Let's load up the plane and get the Geccos on their way before they start losing daylight."

A few minutes later all our gear was on the plane and we were about to board when a familiar voice bellowed, "Stay out of trouble, Hardys!"

We turned around to see a familiar figure trudging toward

the river in a very unfamiliar outfit. Bayport's top cop looked downright goofy wearing a floppy fishing hat and rubber waders instead of his chief-of-police uniform.

"Looking spiffy, Chief Olaf," Joe chirped, unable to hide his smirk.

"If you're half as good at catching fish as you are at catching criminals, then those aquatic vertebrates won't stand a chance, sir," I added, causing Joe to nearly spit on himself trying not to laugh.

"I should have known better than to take my vacation in the same place as the Hardy boys," Chief Olaf grumbled. "As if you two don't get in my way enough already in Bayport!"

The chief likes to gives us a hard time—and, to be fair, our stellar detective work does kind of tend to make the police look bad—but he's actually a nice guy beneath the grumpy exterior.

"You're the reason I need a vacation in the first place!" The chief's fishing rod wiggled as he jabbed it in our direction. "You boys do anything to disrupt my fishing trip and you'll be going back to Bayport in cuffs."

"Happy hunting, Chief!" Joe called after him as the chief plodded toward the water, sighing and muttering to himself.

It wasn't long before we were buckled in and ready for take-off. Commander Gonzo had taxied the little plane right up next to the lodge so there'd be enough room to take off using the field as a runway.

"All right, kiddies!" our pilot shouted to be heard over the plane's engine and whirling propeller. "I gotta run back in to use the little boys' room. Anybody forgot anything, now's the time to get it. You don't want to get out in the bush and find out you left behind your tents and toilet paper."

"I'm pretty sure we have everything," Jim said meekly as he checked and double-checked his seat belt.

"Wait!" I shouted. "I forgot my research journal!"

After reading Dr. Kroopnik's last article, I'd come up with some field research ideas of my own that I was eager to share with him.

"Please hurry, Frank," Jim pleaded, looking more and more green by the minute. "The sooner we take off, the sooner we can get out of this sardine can."

"I love sardines!" Commander Gonzo declared in nonsensical delight as he hopped off the plane and marched back to the lodge ahead of me. I ran back inside to the room Joe and I were sharing, grabbed my notebook, and was on my way back to the plane when I heard the muffled sound of a whispered argument through a cracked door at the back of the lodge. With the noisy plane right outside distorting and drowning out the words, I couldn't tell who was talking or understand much of anything they were saying. It sounded like only one voice talking, though. I didn't mean to eavesdrop, but, well—I am a detective, after all.

I put my ear up to the door and strained to decipher what the hushed voice was saying. I could just barely piece together one angry whisper—and I immediately wished I hadn't.

"It's too dangerous," the voice mumbled. "No one knows about the crazy hermit in the woods. . . . I don't want anyone else getting hurt."

THIS IS YOUR COMMANDER SPEAKING

3

JOE

ALL RIGHT, FOLKS, BUCKLE UP AND brace yourselves, because this bucket of bolts is about to go airborne!" Commander Gonzo announced as Frank climbed back on the plane, looking nearly as ill as our teacher.

I figured Frank was just as nervous as everyone else about flying in the tiny plane with the Commander—with only one propeller, seven seats, and a crazy man in the cockpit, this definitely wasn't a first-class flight. I couldn't help being a little excited, though. I mean, talk about a thrill ride!

Frank tried to get my attention from his seat next to Randall, but Commander Gonzo piped up before he could say anything.

"Let's see if this old puddle jumper still has any hop,"

Gonzo shouted as the plane started rumbling its way across the field on two wheels.

The plane picked up speed, bouncing us around in our seats like jumping beans with every bump in the ground. If it weren't for the seat belts, we'd be ricocheting all over the cabin.

Jim had his eyes shut and his face was white; Mandy and Melissa had a death grip on each other's forearms; and Frank was looking out the window back at the lodge with that *I hope I'm wrong, but I'm pretty sure the world is coming to an end* look he gets sometimes.

"This better be worth it," Randall whimpered.

The wooden fence at the edge of the field closed in on us so fast, I started to wonder if the plane would have enough room to lift off. I wasn't really worried, though.

At least not until our pilot shouted, "We're not gonna make it!"

All seven of us screamed at the same time as the plane's wheels lifted off the ground and the tin bird took flight, clearing the fence by mere inches.

"Whoo-hoo!" Commander Gonzo shouted. "I love that part!"

He turned around in his seat with a big grin and held out a can of peanuts. "Anybody want a snack?"

We were all so relieved to be alive, we started laughing hysterically. Although I'm not totally sure about Jim; it was hard to tell if he was laughing or hyperventilating.

"So is 'commander' just a different way of saying 'captain'?" Mandy asked, scooping out a handful of peanuts.

"Lieutenant, actually," he said, pointing to the military insignia sewn crookedly onto his floppy hat. "Flight Commander Gonzo Gonzales, US Air Force, retired, at your service. But you can call me Doc."

"Wow, so you're a doctor as well as a pilot?" Melissa asked.

"Nah, the boys in my squadron used to call me that because of all the bones I broke flying for Uncle Sam. Said I spent so much time in the infirmary getting patched up, I might as well have a medical degree."

"Uh, is it normal to break bones flying an airplane?" Jim asked shakily.

"It is when you fly the way I used to!" Gonzo replied proudly.

Jim groaned.

"Don't worry," he reassured our teacher. "I haven't crashed in decades."

Doc tipped back the can of nuts and chugged a mouthful, talking as he chewed. "Can't say that for some other pilots around here, though. Flying this mountain range can be tricky if you don't have skills like mine. A little Cessna—the exact same model as this one—went down on Black Bear Mountain right near where you folks are going, as a matter of fact."

"I'm never flying again," Jim muttered.

"You're talking about that Russian guy, right?" Randall asked, perking up. "My parents told me about him."

"Yup, it was big news around here when it happened about thirty years ago. Aleksei Orlov. Guy had a huge ole mansion with miles of exotic gardens and his own private zoo and stuff downstate. Big-time player in the Russian 'Mafiya,' they said. Died in a ball of flames on the mountainside before the Feds got a chance to take him to trial. Turned out he was a better mobster than a pilot, I guess."

"I heard that he—" Randall began, but Frank cut him off.

"Does anybody actually live on Black Bear Mountain? Besides Dr. Kroopnik, I mean," he asked Gonzo, speaking up for the first time since takeoff. From how nervous he sounded, I guessed he was probably still feeling a little queasy about the flight.

"You mean like are there any crazy old mountain men stalking about in the woods up there?" Doc Gonzo asked.

Frank's eyes went wide. "Um, yeah, kind of."

"Sure are!" Gonzo exclaimed.

All our eyes went a little wide at that one.

"You hear all kinds of stories about hermits spending their whole lives living off the grid out here because of how remote it is," he explained. "I wouldn't worry about it too much, though. I haven't heard about them eating any campers." He paused to pick a peanut from his teeth before adding, "At least not for a few years."

I was about to ask Gonzo to elaborate when the plane

crested a ridge and Black Bear Mountain rose into the sky ahead of us. The mist-shrouded summit loomed over all the other mountains below like something out of a storybook. I almost wouldn't have been surprised if a dragon had appeared and started shooting fireballs at us!

"Thar she blows!" Doc Gonzo called. "If you had reclining seat backs or tray tables, I'd tell you to put them in their upright and locked positions, because we'll be on the ground in just about a minute."

Gonzo swept the plane down toward a large clearing high up on the mountain. Even higher than that, we caught a glimpse of an old cabin perched atop wooden stilts on the edge of a ravine, overlooking a gnarly set of river rapids rushing down the mountainside below.

"That must be Dr. Kroopnik's research station," Frank said.

"Yes, that's the old ranger lookout cabin he's using," Jim said. "You see how it has windows all the way around? That gave rangers a three-hundred-and-sixty-degree view, so they could spot any forest fires."

Luckily, Commander Gonzo's landing was less terrifying than his takeoff, and we were safely back on the ground in no time.

"That's the trailhead there where you're supposed to rendezvous with your scientist," Gonzo said, pointing to a path through the dense forest at the edge of the clearing as we finished unloading our gear. "I'll be back for you in seventy-two hours. In the meantime, if you need anything—well, don't, 'cause you're on your own for the next three days."

Gonzo climbed back into his plane and was about to close the door when he spun back around. "Oh, I almost forgot. Whatever you do, don't feed the bears!"

Commander Doc Gonzo slammed the door, fired up the Cessna, and took off, leaving us Geccos to conquer Black Bear Mountain on our own.

"Bears?" whimpered Randall.

"Well, that was interesting," I said cheerily.

"I'm just glad to be back on the ground in one piece," Jim said not so cheerily. "We've still got a few minutes until Dr. Kroopnik is supposed to meet us, so we—"

He was interrupted by the sound of a horse neighing from the woods beyond the trailhead.

"Huh, I guess that must be Dr. Kroopnik now," Jim proclaimed. "I bet he's just as eager to meet us as we are to meet him. He . . ."

Only *he* wasn't. I think we'd all been expecting the esteemed field biologist Dr. Max Kroopnik, PhD, be to your typical nerdy middle-aged scientist guy. But the person who appeared before us, well . . .

"You must be Jim and his conservation club," said the beautiful young woman who came riding out of the woods to greet us. "I'm Max Kroopnik."

BEAR BAIT 4

FRANK

I T'S NICE TO FINALLY MEET YOU," THE GOR-geous blonde said as she climbed gracefully down from her horse.

We were all still too stunned to reply.

"But you're a, um, you're a . . . ," Jim fumbled.

"Yes?" she asked, letting him squirm.

"Well, what I mean to say is, well, we were kind of expecting—"

"You're not a dude!" Joe blurted.

"I'm glad it's that obvious," she said with a laugh, winking at Mandy and Melissa. "Thankfully, that's usually a mistake people only make before they meet me. Maybe it'll help if I reintroduce myself."

She extended her hand to Jim. "Dr. Max 'Don't you dare call me Maxine' Kroopnik. Nice to meet you."

"Jim, um, M-Morgan," Jim stuttered as he shook her hand. "It's, uh, very nice to meet you too, Dr. Kroopnik."

"You can just call me Max," she said.

"Okay, Max." Jim grinned goofily. "I like your bag!"

Max gave him a quizzical look.

"I mean your backpack," he said, pointing to the tan rucksack slung over her shoulder. "You have good taste." There was an awkward moment of silence before he proudly lifted his own identical tan rucksack. "See? We have the same bag!"

"Huh, what are the odds?" she said, sounding less impressed than I think Jim had hoped. If I didn't know better, I'd think our teacher might already have a little crush on our scientist.

"I think it's great that you're a girl," Mandy said.

"Me too!" Max agreed.

"I mean, with so much gender inequality in the scientific community, it's inspiring to see a woman making as big of an impact as you are," Mandy elaborated.

"Oh, um, yeah, thanks," Max mumbled, like she was embarrassed by the compliment.

"Thank you so much for inviting us to come out here to assist with your research," I said. "We're huge fans of all the great conservation work you've done."

"Yeah, uh, actually, I have some bad news for you,"

she said, not meeting our eyes. "Something has come up and, well, I'm not going to be able to let you help with my research after all."

I felt like I'd been sucker punched in the gut. No research?

"B-but you said in your letter—" Jim stammered.

"I'm sorry about that, but I have some very important work to do, and I'm just not going to have the time."

"But can't we at least just observe?" I pleaded.

"We won't get in the way, we promise!" Mandy chimed in.

"I'm sorry to have to let you down like this, but it's just not possible," Max said.

"This is bogus!" Randall protested. "My parents spent a ton of money for us to come out here so I could tell colleges I worked with you."

"What, you want a recommendation or something?" she asked Randall, sounding relieved. "Fine. Leave me your addresses and I'll send recommendations for all of you. You've gone to a lot of trouble to come out here. It's the least I can do."

I couldn't believe it! Dr. Kroopnik was really serious about not letting us work with her! We'd come all the way to see her and she thought it was cool to just send us packing with a stupid letter as a consolation prize? Sure, I was still a little freaked out about the "crazy hermit" stuff I'd overheard back at the lodge, but conducting field research with a renowned scientist was too good an opportunity to pass up. Besides, it was silly to get worked up over a garbled snippet of a conversation I'd probably taken out of context anyway. And like Joe said, the Hardy boys never back down from a challenge.

"I don't care about a college recommendation," I said to Max. "We came here because we wanted to learn from your experience as a field biologist."

"Sorry, kid, it's not going to happen this time," she said sympathetically. "I can help you guys set up camp for the night nearby, and then I'll use the radio at the research station to call the plane back for you first thing in the morning."

"What?" Joe sputtered. "We don't even get to stay and camp?"

"Don't worry, Joe," Jim said. "I'm not getting back on that plane a second sooner than I have to. Just because we won't be able to help Dr. Kroopnik with her research doesn't mean we can't still make the most of our time here."

"I don't think that's a good idea," she said. "I really think it would be better for everybody if you just left in the morning."

"Like you said, we've gone to a lot of trouble to come here," Jim reminded her. "And I don't intend to let my kids down any more than necessary. We've got three full days' worth of provisions, and I've got plenty of great science projects I've been itching to put to the test outside the classroom."

"But—" Max tried to protest, but Jim cut her off.

"Thank you, Dr. Kroopnik, but if you can lead us to our campsite, I can take it from there."

We followed behind Max, who led her horse along a narrow deer trail through the dense forest. With no visible landmarks to help get your bearings, it would be easy to find yourself lost in the woods if you wandered off the winding trail.

We may not have been able to assist her like we'd planned, but I was still hoping to pick Dr. Kroopnik's brain during the little time we did have with her.

"I was really impressed with your last article in *American Scientist*, and I was wondering what kind of methods you used," I said.

"Methodical ones," she quipped.

I was trying to figure out if she was brushing me off or just pulling my leg when Mandy called out from behind us.

"Hey, guys, look at this!"

Mandy leaned over by the side of the trail, where she'd spotted a tiny, cool-looking orange-speckled salamander sitting on a leaf.

"Hey, Max, what kind of salamander is this?" she asked.

"A little one," Max said, barely glancing back. "Now let's get a move on. We're burning daylight."

"Wait a second," I said, leaning down next to Mandy to get a better look. "That looks like one of the endangered salamanders from your study on population decline in mountain-dwelling amphibians. I can't believe we saw a live specimen! They must be making a comeback."

"Huh, yeah," she said absently as she peered over my shoulder. "Good eye, kid. I'll be sure to make a note of it."

She clicked her tongue to get her horse moving and resumed guiding it down the trail without looking back.

Mandy and I exchanged a *what gives?* look. Max was obviously distracted by whatever important new work she was doing. I guess when you study this stuff for a living like Dr. Kroopnik did, seeing another endangered salamander just seems like no big deal. It was still pretty disappointing that she didn't share our enthusiasm, though.

Dr. Kroopnik led us off the trail along a twisty path through the woods to an open space beneath a canopy of tall trees with a fire pit in the center of it.

"You'll set up camp here," she said. "We don't have much daylight, so you'll want to get your tents up and start gathering wood for the fire."

Max knew her way around a campsite, I'll give her that. She moved faster than the rest of us put together, and with her help we had our tents up and a fire burning in no time.

Randall had skipped out on most of the hard work and was sitting on a log, roasting a hot dog on a stick. When the last dog in the package was gone, he carelessly tossed the wrapper over his shoulder.

"Pack it in, pack it out, Randall," Melissa chastised him, reminding him of the conservationist camping motto to always take your trash with you in the wilderness.

"And remember what Gonzo said about feeding the bears," Joe added. "You don't want a big old black bear following a trail of crumbs to your tent and mistaking you for a weenie."

Responsible camping practices may not have motivated Randall, but the thought of turning into a meal for a hungry bear sure did. He had the wrapper off the ground quicker than you could say "late-night snack."

"That's right!" I said. Joe may have been joking, but he reminded me of one of the most important rules of camping in critter country. "We almost forgot to hang up all our food off the ground so the scent doesn't lure any bears into camp during the night."

"For real?" Mandy and Melissa squeaked in unison.

"Black bears rarely pose a threat to people," I informed them. "But they are opportunistic scavengers, and their sense of smell is one of the most acute on earth, so it's best not to tempt them with the promise of a free meal when you're in their territory. And I'm guessing Black Bear Mountain didn't get its name by accident."

That sure got everyone's attention. There wasn't a speck of food left anywhere in camp by the time we were done bundling it all together. Joe and I got to work suspending the bundle ten feet off the ground between two trees with rope, like we'd been taught in wilderness survival boot camp.

"So what about that plane crash?" Randall, who had once again managed to avoid lifting a finger while everyone else did the work, asked Max.

The question caught Max off guard, and she eyed Randall suspiciously. "What plane crash?"

"You know, the one from a long time ago with that Russian mobster guy," he said. "It was near here, right?"

"Yeah!" Joe jumped in, turning to our teacher. "Jim, can we go explore the crash site? How cool would that be?!"

"I have to admit, despite my fear of flying, I am curious," Jim agreed. "Do you know where it is, Max?"

"Ha!" she scoffed. "That's just what I need, a bunch of kids wandering around lost in the woods, mucking up my research. I don't mean to be rude, but if you insist on staying, I suggest you stick to your camp. It's a lot safer."

The light had started to fade quickly, giving the woods an eerie glow as the sun disappeared. I'd managed to put the thing I'd overheard about the crazy hermit out of my mind, but Max's comment about the woods being unsafe had me feeling unsettled all over again.

"You haven't heard of any, like, hermits or anything living in the woods around here, have you?" I asked tentatively.

Max looked up from the fire, fear flashing across her face. Uncomfortable silence descended on the camp as she stared at me for a lot longer than I liked. When she finally spoke, she sounded dead serious.

"In these mountains, it's not the bears you have to worry about eating you."

GHOST STORIES 5

JOE

T WAS LIKE DUSK SUDDENLY GOT TWO shades darker as soon as Max spoke. She was the second person that day to reference hermits and cannibalism in the same sentence. I'd assumed Gonzo had only been joking on the plane when he'd mentioned hermits eating campers, but it sure didn't sound like Max was.

The rest of us shut up and sat down on logs around the fire. Max took her time, firelight flickering across her face, distorting her pretty features as she shifted her gaze from one Gecco to the next like she was sizing us up to see if we were ready to hear what she had to say.

In the silence, the sounds of the wilderness around us seemed to come to life—and not in a good way.

AARROOOOOOOOOO!

Shivers shot straight down my spine as the high-pitched howl of a hungry beast pierced the evening. Randall practically jumped off his log, and the Ms clung to each other for dear life. The sun had set and the coyotes had risen.

Max laughed, but there wasn't any humor to it.

"It's not the coyotes you have to worry about either," she said. "Take a seat. What I'm about to tell you just might save your lives."

We were already hanging on every word.

"I love a good campfire ghost story." Jim chuckled nervously.

"Some stories are more than just legends," she said, fixing him with a hard stare before shifting her gaze to me. "You know that plane crash you were so eager to see?"

"Uh-huh," I gulped.

"Well, there's a reason they never found any survivors."

"The Russian guy burned up in the crash, right?" Randall asked timidly.

"That was the official story," Max said. "What they wanted people to think so they wouldn't be scared off. But not everything about that crash made the news. You see, in places like this, out here in the middle of nowhere, the local economy relies on people like you who pay good money to escape the city for a little fresh air and outdoor fun. Well, let's just say the local authorities know when something isn't good for business. And who wants to go camping or fishing or hiking when they know there's a bloodthirsty—" Max stopped midsentence and took a deep breath.

"But I'm getting ahead of myself," she said, leaving us hanging so close to the edge of our seats, I nearly fell off.

"What they didn't tell the press is that they did find forensic evidence—just one small piece," she continued. "A single charred bone fragment from a human toe. From the way the bone had been chewed on, they could tell that its former owner had been hungrily devoured."

"It was probably just scavengers getting an easy meal after the poor guy died in the wreck," Frank said, trying to reassure us with the most logical explanation before Max got a chance to hit us with whatever awful punch line she had in store.

"Sure, that's what they thought too," she said. "Until they got it back to the lab and examined the tooth marks more closely. The victim had been eaten by a wild beast, all right. Only this wild beast had human teeth."

All six of us gasped at the same time.

"Locals had always suspected there were still mountain people living in the remotest parts of the woods. Hikers had been disappearing for years, and there were rumors that they'd fallen prey to a feral beast of a man known as the Mad Hermit of Black Bear Mountain—campfire stories, as you quaintly called them," Max said, turning to Jim. "But it wasn't until they found that gruesome piece of gnarled human bone that people realized the legend of the Mad Hermit was real."

There was a sudden snap as an ember popped in the fire, nearly causing us to jump out of our seats.

"The reason they never found the victims from that plane crash thirty years ago?" Max continued as the sparks rose into the air. "The crazed mountain man who patrols the very mountaintop where we're now camped roasted them over a fire just like this one, and then he ate them."

"Okay, uh, great story!" Jim cut Max off, trying to force his grimace into a strained smile. "Now, who's up for singing some happy campfire songs?"

Max ignored him, turning to us instead. "I promise you it's not a story."

Jim cleared his throat conspicuously, cutting Max off again before she could say anything else. "Okay, thank you, Max. I think that's enough for one night."

No one else had uttered a peep. Randall looked like he wanted to curl up into a ball and disappear. Mandy and Melissa were gripping each other's hands so hard, their knuckles had turned white. And even Frank, who's usually the first one to chime in with a scientific myth-busting analysis of a tall tale, looked terrified. I think that's what scared me more than anything. If my brother thought Max was telling the truth . . .

"It's just a campfire tale, guys," Jim said, trying to reassure us. "It's a scary one, I'll give Max that, but I can assure you it's just an outrageous story."

"Is it really so outrageous?" Max challenged him, her tone as serious as ever. "Black Bear Mountain is one of the most remote wildernesses left in the lower forty-eight states. A person could spend their entire life living off the land up here without anyone else ever knowing. Someone who was a loner. Rejected by civilized society. Unstable, maybe even deranged."

"I don't think—" Jim tried to interject, but Max didn't give him a chance.

"But here's the thing: live alone in the woods without any human contact for long enough and you start to go mad, even if you weren't that way to begin with. And, well, if you live your entire life surviving on nothing but bush meat and berries, that kind of person might just get excited about a little variety in their diet. Especially something exotic. Like human fle—"

"That's enough!" Jim stood up. "This is incredibly unprofessional of you, Dr. Kroopnik. You're taking this too far, and I don't find it funny at all."

"Good. You're not supposed to," Max replied, calmly getting up from the fire and brushing herself off. "There's a reason people tend to go missing on Black Bear Mountain, and you'd all do well to keep an eye out for him while you're here. Better scared and alive than oblivious and dinner."

With that, Max grabbed the rucksack at her feet and turned to leave.

"Sleep tight, kids," she called over her shoulder without looking back. "I'll be making camp right on the other side of that spruce grove. I'm in the middle of some field research that requires my observation all day and night, so

I'm staying in the woods for a few days. If you need anything, just scream."

"Jim," Mandy said softly once Max had left. "I want to go home."

Melissa nodded vigorously. "Can we have Max radio for the plane to come back? Please?"

Jim looked crestfallen. "Come on, guys, it was just a story. Getting to experience the pristine beauty of places like this is what our club is all about. Don't you want the chance to really take advantage of it?"

"I want to explore and all," Melissa said, "but maybe we can just go back to the lodge and tag along with that ranger guy Steven and Casey know instead. That would be just as good, right?"

"There's nothing to worry about, I promise," Jim said, trying his best to sound confident. "It wasn't very nice of her, but I think Max was just trying to scare you, that's all. We're not going to let a silly little ghost story ruin our whole trip, right, guys?"

Jim looked at us expectantly. Randall was too busy being terrified and muttering to himself to voice an opinion. Me, I wasn't sure what to think about the whole thing. Jim was probably right and it was likely just a story, but man, Max was one heck of a storyteller. My instinct was never to back down from a challenge, and that included not running away from an awesome camping adventure just because someone told us a creepy bedtime story. But that someone also happened to be a credible world-renowned scientist with, like, twenty-five degrees, and I'd be lying if I said I wasn't totally freaked out.

"What do you think, Frank?" Jim turned to my brother. "Help me reassure the Geccos there's nothing to worry about."

"I . . ." Frank hesitated. "I don't know."

Well, that sure didn't help—now I really was worried. Frank was about to say something else, but then he looked over at the girls and seemed to think better of it.

"Listen, guys," Jim said. "Organizing this trip was a lot of work, and I'm not going to let a flaky scientist with a bad sense of humor ruin it. Trust me, everyone will feel a lot better when the sun comes up in the morning. Now let's all try to get some rest. We've had a long day. We'll be laughing about this over my famous flapjack breakfast in the morning, you'll see!"

"Jim's right, guys, we'll all be laughing at his cooking in the morning," I joked to Mandy, hoping to lighten the mood—and hoping I was right!—as we went back to our tents.

"Thanks, Joe," she said with a little smile. "I don't know how much sleep I'll be getting, though."

Back in our tent, Frank dropped a bomb on me.

"I didn't say anything before because I didn't want to freak everyone else out even more, but I overheard something back at the lodge that I think you should hear too."

I sat there with my mouth open as he relayed the snippet

of muffled argument he'd overheard about a crazy hermit in the woods and us being in danger.

"You're usually the one trying to convince me monsters aren't real!" I said.

"There's probably a perfectly rational explanation," he said wishfully. "I could barely make out what the person was whispering over all the noise from the plane. I could have misheard or they could have been talking about something else altogether, but after what Commander Gonzo said and now Max, well . . ."

"The coincidence is too great to ignore," I agreed, finishing his thought.

Frank nodded. "I'd feel better if we slept in shifts tonight so one of us can keep an ear out, just in case."

"So do we try to talk Jim into leaving again in the morning?" I asked.

"No, I'm with him on that one," Frank replied. "I've been too excited to see Dr. Kroopnik's research ecosystem to just turn around, even if I do have to study it on my own without her help. Besides, my detective senses are tingling, and I kinda want to stick around to see what happens next."

"I'm with you, bro. I'll take first shift. You try to get some rest."

Jim had been right about at least one thing—it had been a long day, all right. I barely made it ten minutes into my watch before I was sound asleep, dreaming of zip lines and white-water rapids and motorboats and . . . wait, what?

I woke up to Frank snoring so loudly it was like listening to an outboard engine in need of a tune-up.

"Dude," I mumbled groggily, elbowing his sleeping bag. "Wake up, bro. If you snore any louder, you're gonna give the whole camp tinnitus."

"Whuh?" he grumbled. "I thought that was you."

"No, man, I . . ."

Wait a second! Now we were both awake, and the snoring sound had only gotten louder.

"What the—?"

"*AAAHHHHHHHHHHH!*" The girls' screams tore through the campsite before I could finish my thought, jolting us out of our sleeping bags.

"Mandy! Melissa!" I yelled, yanking open the tent flap.

That's when I realized it wasn't snores we'd been hearing. Silhouetted against the first light of dawn in the center of camp stood an enormous black bear.

BEAR RAID 6

FRANK

JOE AND I JUMPED INTO ACTION AT the same time. We dashed out of the tent hollering and waving our hands over our heads to make ourselves look as intimidating as possible. Well, at least as intimidating as a pair of teenage guys can be while facing off against an apex predator that weighed nearly twice as much as both of us combined!

When we got out of the tent, we saw more than just a giant bear. We also saw all our food—or what was left of it. The bundle we'd carefully hung in the trees had been torn open, and the food that hadn't already been devoured by the bear was now scattered around the center of camp.

The bear looked up from its early breakfast and let out a ferocious roar. Every bone in my body told me to run in the opposite direction, but I forced myself to stand my ground.

"Go get your own grub!" I yelled, waving my hands high over my head to make myself seem bigger, like we'd been taught.

"Back off, Bear Boy!" Joe added, picking up a stick and waving it in the bear's direction.

Black bears are fearsome predators, but we were counting on the fact that they rarely attack people. They usually go out of their way to avoid them, actually. But they love free food as much as the next guy and aren't afraid to invade a campsite for an easy meal. By trying to make ourselves seem as threatening as possible, we were hoping to convince our uninvited guest that this meal might not be so easy after all. Besides, running away is just about the worst thing you can do when confronted with a hungry predator—it triggers the animal's chase instinct and makes you seem like prey.

Apparently, no one had told Randall that, because he was sprinting as fast as he could toward Max's campsite. Luckily for Randall, the bear was too bewildered by the scene we were making to pay any attention. It gave a snort in our direction and wandered back out of the camp.

"And don't let the door hit you in the bear butt on your way out!" Joe added for good measure.

The Ms ran out of their tent toward us.

"Thank you so much," Melissa said. "I thought for sure that bear was going to eat us next!"

My mishap on the zip line may not have impressed Melissa, but judging from how tightly she hugged me, our standoff with the bear sure did the trick.

"You must not have done a very good job of tying your food up," Max commented. Randall cowered behind her as she walked into camp and eyed the mess left by the bear.

"But we did!" I said. "I double-checked the knots myself. Everything was securely tied up in the trees when we went to sleep."

Melissa and Mandy seemed a lot less concerned with how the food had gotten down than they were with getting the heck out of there.

"Can you go call the plane back now?" Melissa begged Max. "I don't want to wait until morning."

"Yeah!" Mandy agreed. "Get us as far away from that bear as possible!"

Max looked at the first signs of dawn lightening the sky through the treetops. "Fine by me. Tell your teacher to come out of hiding and I'll head up to the station to radio the lodge while you break down camp."

"Where is Jim, anyway?" I asked, realizing we hadn't seen him at all during the whole bear ordeal.

"He's probably still cowering in his sleeping bag," Max snickered.

"That doesn't sound like Jim to me," Joe said. "He may not be the most graceful guy in the world, but he wouldn't just hide while we were in danger."

"Hey, Jim," Max called out. "The big bad bear is gone. You can come out now!"

When no one replied, Joe and I shot each other a look and headed for his tent. I started to get a sinking feeling when I saw the open flap swaying in the breeze.

"Jim?" I said, pulling back the flap the rest of the way.

"He's gone!" Joe gasped as we peered inside the empty tent.

"City slickers," Max muttered derisively. "Figures he'd get scared and run off."

"His pack is gone too," Randall cried. "He left us!"

"No way. Jim wouldn't have . . ." Joe paused and pointed to something on the tent floor. "Hey, what's that?"

I turned on my flashlight to get a better look—but only for a second. Choking back a gasp, I quickly switched it off again. I just hoped I'd been fast enough to keep our classmates from seeing the dark red streak of what looked like blood on the floor of our teacher's tent.

STRANDED 7

JOE

THE BEAR GOT HIM!" MANDY CRIED, grabbing hold of Melissa's arm.

Frank had tried to turn off the light in time to prevent anyone from panicking, but the one quick glimpse of red had been plenty.

"It ate Jim!" Melissa wailed.

"I don't think so," Frank said grimly, turning the flashlight back on and shining it at the ground around us. "There are plenty of human footprints, but no bear tracks anywhere near the tent."

Frank's light swept over the campsite, illuminating the giant paw prints among the scattered remains of broken eggs and flapjack mix and the chewed-up bundle that used to hold it all. I walked over and picked up an end of the cord we'd used to hoist it into the tree. I expected to find the cord chewed up too, like maybe the bear had outwitted us to get at the food. But it wasn't chewed or even frayed at all.

"It's severed cleanly." I held up the end of the rope for Frank to see. "Like somebody sliced it with a knife."

"Why are you guys wasting time worrying about the stupid rope?" Randall whined. "We need to find Jim!"

"Because somebody could have cut it on purpose," Frank said, drawing the same frightening conclusion I had. "Almost like they wanted the bear to come into our camp."

"But why would anyone want to do that?" Mandy asked in disbelief.

The Ms and Randall looked perplexed. Max seemed to get it, though—our close call with the bear hadn't frazzled her at all, but when she realized Jim was gone, she started to sweat.

"A bear rampaging through camp might create a heck of a diversion," I theorized, really hoping I was wrong.

"And the zipper on Jim's tent isn't just open, it's torn," Frank added, shining his light on the tent flap, which was streaked with red like the floor. "Like there was a struggle."

Melissa chewed anxiously on her bottom lip. "You don't really think someone meant for the bear to come into camp so they could take Jim, do you?"

"His tent is the farthest from the fire and closest to the woods," I said, peering into the shadowy forest beyond the tent. "It would have made him the easiest target if someone did."

"What if they plan to come back and pick us off one by one, like in the movies?" Randall whined.

"But that's crazy!" Mandy cried. "Who would want to do such a thing?!"

The answer hit us all at the same time. The girls gasped, Randall whimpered, and Max's hand reflexively shot down to the handle of the knife she wore on her hip.

"What if the Mad Hermit of Black Bear Mountain is real?" Frank murmured.

"Everyone stay right here," Max commanded before we had a chance to react to Frank's terrifying suggestion. "I'm going to find your teacher."

"Don't leave us!" Mandy pleaded, grabbing her arm.

"Everything is going to be fine," Max tried to reassure us, but from the way she was scanning the woods with her eyes, she was obviously on high alert. "He probably just got scared off by the bear and got himself lost. Stay put and I'll be back with Jim in an hour, by the time the sun is all the way up."

She turned and stalked back to her camp before anyone had a chance to protest.

"Stupid amateur campers," I heard her grumble as she left. "I'm supposed to be a scientist, not a babysitter."

Max rode out of camp a few minutes later, calling over her shoulder, "One hour!"

But two hours later, she was still gone. Three hours later, the awful reality hit us.

We were stranded alone in the wilderness. No adults, no way to call for help, and, quite possibly, a killer on the loose.

HUNTED 8

FRANK

"WE'RE ALL GOING TO DIE!" RANDALL wailed, burying his face in his hands.

"We're not going to die, Randall," I said firmly before his hysteria had a chance to spread—I just hoped I sounded more confident about it than I felt. "We just need to stay calm and come up with a plan."

"Yeah, don't be so dramatic, Randall," Melissa said, trying to put on a brave face. "Frank and Joe must deal with this kind of thing all the time in their detective work, right, guys?"

Melissa and Mandy looked at us expectantly. Sure, Joe and I have gotten out of some tight spots, but being stranded on a remote mountaintop with a mad cannibal wasn't one of them.

"We don't need detectives," Randall moaned. "We need an airplane!"

"You're right, and we're going to signal for one," Joe said. "One of the first things we need to do is build a signal fire that can be seen from the air to alert any passing planes that we're in distress."

"That's our best bet," I agreed. "Since Jim's bag has the maps and the GPS, we're not going to be able to hike anywhere for help without getting lost and making it harder for someone to find us."

I looked up at the dense canopy of trees shading our campsite. "A couple of us are going to have to go on a short scouting mission, though. We need to find a better location to build a fire. That will also give us a chance to scope out the terrain and see if we can spot Max's ranger station to radio for help."

"No way," Mandy protested. "We are not splitting up."

"Yeah, every time someone leaves the camp, they don't come back!" Melissa added.

"Frank's right, guys," Joe said gently. "Normally, the best thing to do in this kind of situation would be for everyone to stay where they are and wait for rescue, but our camp is too densely wooded to signal for help. And thanks to that bear, we don't have enough food or water to just wait around for three days."

He kicked one of the empty jugs of water the bear had ransacked along with all our grub.

"But can't we all just go together?" Melissa asked.

"I'm sorry, Melissa. We need everyone else to stay here in case Jim and Max come back," I said, looking back up at the storm clouds that had started to roll in. "Besides, we already have fire and shelter here, which are the two most critical things you need for wilderness survival. It would be too dangerous for all of us to go stumbling around the woods without knowing what's out there."

"Or who," Randall said ominously. "No way am I going out there. Not with some crazy killer on the loose."

"How heroic of you, Randall," Mandy sneered.

"Hey, I'd rather be a live chicken than a barbecued hero," he shot back.

"I'll go," Melissa volunteered softly.

"That's really brave of you," I told her. "But Joe and I have the most outdoors training and we work well as a team. It will be the quickest way for us to signal for help and make it back here safely."

"Just stay alert and light the fire again and we'll be back before you know it," Joe said, trying to sound cheery as we left the rest of the Geccos and set out on our own.

We made our way uphill through the woods, figuring higher ground would be our best bet. We looked around carefully, moving as silently as we could to stay off the radar of any hungry predators. And I don't mean bears.

If it were just a matter of being lost in the woods, we probably would have called out for Jim and Max as we went, but the possibility of a Mad Hermit out there waiting to turn us into lunch changed the game.

"There," Joe whispered, pointing through the trees to what looked like a clearing.

"That'll work," I said a minute later as we peered out at a large meadow surrounded by trees. "It doesn't give us much of a view to look for the ranger station, but any planes passing over this side of the mountain should be able to see it."

"It's going to be impossible to stay quiet while we gather wood, so we just have to move as quickly as we can," Joe said, scanning the tree line to make sure we were still alone.

It really stunk that we weren't getting a chance to actually stop and appreciate the mountainside. I normally would have been totally psyched to be somewhere so beautiful and wild—but in our current situation, stranded, with two people missing and the threat of a killer hiding behind every tree, Black Bear Mountain seemed more like a death trap than a nature preserve.

As I reached down to pick up some firewood, I noticed just how cool the forest floor looked. It was like standing on a carpet of funky green moss with patches of tiny blue flowers and feathery green shrubs polka-dotted with bright red and yellow blossoms. All those plants growing together rang a bell in my mental library.

"Hey, check this out," I whispered to Joe. "These plants are indigenous to the mountain ranges of eastern Europe and central Asia! I recognize them from one of the botany books in Jim's classroom."

Joe looked at me like I was insane.

"It's like a patch of forest from Mongolia or Siberia somehow wound up on top of a mountain in America!" I explained. "It could be scientifically significant. I wonder if this is one of the things Max is studying. It would be fascinating to find out how the plants got here and what kind of effect they have on the native ecosystem."

"Leave it to my brother to geek out about local flora while we're being stalked by a crazed cannibal," Joe muttered. "Now let's get this fire started before it starts to rain."

"Oh right, sorry about that," I said with an embarrassed glance up at the darkening sky. "I guess I can get a little overexcited about this kind of nature stuff sometimes."

"I hadn't noticed," Joe said, rolling his eyes. "I was going to suggest making three separate fires in the shape of a triangle like we learned in survival boot camp, but maybe we should just try to get one big one going first before it rains."

Luckily, there were a couple of old downed trees right on the edge of the clearing, which made wood gathering easier. We grabbed some live spruce boughs as well, knowing green wood creates lots of smoke, which would make the fire easier to spot from far away. We piled it all up in the middle of the clearing, away from the trees, so we wouldn't accidentally set a forest fire. The first drops of rain started to plop down around us just as we managed to get it lit.

"If you want to work on feeding the fire, I'll use the extra wood to make a big X on the ground next to it," I told Joe. "That way they there'll still be a distress signal for someone to spot after the fire goes out."

"Sounds like a plan, man. Let's—" Joe stopped mid-sentence and looked up toward the woods. "Did you hear that?"

I froze in place, scanning the tree line and straining to hear any sign that someone might be out there. Suddenly every shadow and rustling branch seemed threatening, but I couldn't see or hear anything out of the usual.

"Sorry, dude, I think I'm just on edge," Joe said after an excruciatingly long minute of silence. "It was probably just a squirrel or something. Let's finish up and get out of here."

As soon as Joe turned back to the fire, the unmistakable sound of a horse neighing snapped our attention right back to the woods.

"That's got to be Max's horse, right?" I asked hopefully.

The horse burst into the clearing, answering the question for us.

It was Max's horse, all right. Only it seemed to have found a new rider—a hairy ax-wielding man covered in tattered animal skins and war paint!

TUNA SURPRISE

9

JOE

NY HOPE I HAD THAT JIM AND MAX were okay vanished as the distance closed between us and the nightmarish figure on Max's horse.

The deranged rider bore down on us in silent fury, ax raised to strike. With all the pelts whipping around, our attacker looked more monster than human, like something a mad scientist had stitched together from pieces of ten different animals! A grimacing bear's head covered the top of the rider's face, a furry beard obscured the bottom, and the skin in between was smeared with black ash and bloodred war paint. Or maybe it was just blood.

The Mad Hermit of Black Bear Mountain apparently *was* real, and it had Max's horse, which meant it probably had Max too. And if we didn't act fast, the Hardy boys were going to be the hermit's next victims.

"Run!" Frank screamed.

Between the hooves thundering against the ground, the actual thunder ripping through the sky, and my heart trying to beat its way out of my chest, I could barely hear him. That didn't stop me from running, though.

Frank sprinted for the woods with me at his heels as the hoofbeats grew louder behind us and the sky opened up, unleashing a torrential downpour. We plowed blindly into the thick brush at the other end of the clearing, where it would be harder for the horse to follow—which would have been great if the clearing hadn't been right on the edge of a hidden gulch.

One second we were running through the woods and the next we were rolling straight down a humongous hill! I tried to grab hold of something to slow myself down, but the hill was too steep, especially with the rain turning everything around us to mud. I tumbled head over heels after my brother, praying we weren't about to roll right off the side of the mountain.

I heard a thump followed by an "Umph!" when Frank hit the bottom and braced myself for impact.

"Oof!" I grunted as I rolled to a surprisingly gentle stop beside my brother. I opened my eyes, hoping I hadn't broken every bone in my body and was in too much shock to realize it. But nope! We'd landed in a huge bed of lush green ferns!

"Huh," Frank said, examining one of the leaves. "This looks like *Dennstaedtia punctilobula*."

"Whatever it's called, it's my new favorite plant," I said. "I thought we were goners for sure."

"We still might be," Frank reminded me, shifting his gaze back up to the top of the hill.

I was so disoriented from our fall, I'd almost forgotten what we'd been running from in the first place! I stared up anxiously, but there was no sign of the Mad Hermit.

"That hill might have saved our lives," Frank said. "Do you think we lost him?"

"I don't know. It's too steep for him to make it down on horseback, but he knows these woods a lot better than we do," I said, squinting to see through the downpour. "Let's find some kind of shelter where we can hide until the rain lets up."

"When in doubt, follow running water downstream," Frank said, recalling another wilderness survival lesson, pointing to the swelling brook running downhill through the ferns. "I bet that eventually feeds into the rapids we saw from the plane beneath the ranger station."

Two good things about being pelted by pouring rain were that it made it easier for us to move silently through the woods and a lot harder for someone to track us. It also made for a pretty miserable hike, though, so I was relieved when I saw the opening to a cave at the base of a rocky ledge.

I pointed it out to Frank, and we approached cautiously in case any wild animals had the same idea about waiting out the storm.

"I can't see more than a few feet in," Frank said as we ducked into the cavern and out of the rain.

"I only have a few matches left," I told him, reaching into my pocket for the little waterproof survival kit I always carry with me while exploring. "But we should at least be able to scope it out to see if it's safe."

Two matches bought us enough light to make it to the back of the cave. It wasn't large, but the back wall was out of sight of the entrance, so there was no way someone was going to be able to spot us, especially not in the pitch black that engulfed us when the second match went out.

"I guess this will have to do," Frank's voice floated out of the darkness. "I . . . OOF!"

I heard Frank stumble to the ground a few feet away.

I crouched into a fighting stance, ready to face an unseen threat in the dark cave.

"You okay, bro?" I asked.

"Yeah, I think I tripped over something. Can you spare another match?"

"Only two more left after this," I said as the match sparked to life in my fingers.

"Weird," Frank said, examining a loop of rope sticking out of the cave's dirt floor.

He gave it a tug and the dirt began to shake loose, uncovering more rope hidden beneath the surface. "There's something down there," he said.

He scooped the dirt away with his hands and gave another big tug. The ground beneath the rope gave way as Frank yanked a rusty metal box to the surface.

"Ouch!" I yelped as the match burned out on my fingertips. I'd been so engrossed in Frank's discovery, I hadn't been paying attention to the match. I quickly lit another.

"Only one more match left," I told Frank, excited to find out what was in the box.

Frank used his pocketknife to pry off the lid. It opened with a groan.

"Is it treasure?" I asked eagerly.

"Not unless you consider expired cans of tuna and beans treasure," Frank said, holding open a box full of rusted cans of food. "Someone must have stashed it here years ago to keep an emergency cache of food somewhere bears couldn't get to."

"Hey, is that tuna fish in oil?" I grabbed one of the cans. "Sweet—it is!"

I could see Frank's face scrunch up in disgust as the match burned out. "I've seen you eat some gross stuff before, Joe, but if you take a single bite of that tuna, I swear I'm gonna puke."

"Trust me, dude," I told him. He couldn't see me grinning in the dark, but I had a plan.

Going by feel, I used the awl on my Swiss Army knife to punch a hole in the top of the can. Then I cut a couple of inches of cord from the small roll I keep in my survival kit and jammed it in the hole in the top of the can, making sure to get the makeshift wick nice and wet with the fishy oil.

"Here goes nothing," I said as I sparked my final match to life and held it against the cord.

The match flickered and fizzed, and for a second I didn't think it was going to work, but the cord not only lit, it stayed lit! Our cave was dark no longer.

"Behold!" I announced. "It's a tuna torch!"

"I never thought I'd say this about something that smells like burning rotten fish, but that is awesome," Frank said. "With all the oil in the can, that could probably burn for an hour."

"Now that we have light, let's try to figure out what the heck is going on," I said. "I know I came on this trip for adventure, but facing off with bears and hiding from cannibals in caves is too much, even for me."

"Maybe we'll get lucky and someone will have seen the smoke from our signal fire before it went out," Frank said. "Do you think the rest of the Geccos are all right?"

"I guess the one good thing about the Mad Hermit coming after us is that it keeps him away from them, for a while at least," I offered. "I don't know if we could even find our way back to camp if we tried. I think our best bet is to look for the research station and call for help."

Frank nodded solemnly. "I don't even want to think about what may have happened to Jim and Max."

It sounded like the rain had begun to let up a little, and another noise started to echo into the cave from somewhere outside. It sounded a lot like snoring.

"Uh-oh," I squeaked as it dawned on me that we might have unwittingly sent an odoriferous invitation to a very unwanted guest.

"The tuna torch!" Frank gasped.

I quickly blew out the flame, but I had a feeling the damage had been done. Turned out there was one major problem with our DIY candle: it reeked of stinky fish. And judging from the snorting and grunting coming from the mouth of the cave, bears love stinky fish.

The high-pitched scream we heard next definitely didn't come from a bear, though. We ran to the front of the cave to discover that the bear wasn't alone.

Jim was alive!

Our soaking-wet teacher cowered just outside the cave with his tattered rucksack cradled to his chest—and he was standing face-to-face with what looked like the same humongous bear that had ransacked our camp earlier!

Jim shrieked. The bear yelped. And the equally terrified bear and teacher turned to run as fast as they could in opposite directions. Only Jim ran smack-dab into the cave wall, knocking himself out cold.

And that wasn't even the most surprising thing! It was the huge stack of partially burned money that fell out of Jim's bag after he hit the ground.

IN DEMANTOID 10

FRANK

"H E'S ALIVE!" I CRIED, LOOKING DOWN at Jim and the bundle of strange-looking charred currency now lying by his side. The showdown between the bear, our teacher, and the cave wall had me shocked, elated, and baffled all at once.

"And he's rich!" Joe added, reaching down to pick up the cash. "I've never seen money like this before."

The bills were about the size of normal paper currency, but they were a pale peachy color with strange foreign writing on them and singed, frayed edges, like someone had tried to light them on fire. "I have no idea what they say, but these are all hundreds." Joe's pupils practically turned into dollar signs as he flipped rapidly through the stack.

"There must be, like, fifty or sixty thousand bucks here!"

I grabbed one of the bills. All the text was printed in a Slavic-looking language I couldn't decipher, maybe Russian or Ukrainian, so the only thing I could read were the numbers. They were hundreds, all right, but instead of Benjamin Franklin, they had a picture of an old bald dude with a pointy goatee.

"Too bad these are Lenins instead of Franklins." I pointed to the large drawing of Communist Party founder Vladimir Ilyich Lenin. "These must be rubles from before the collapse of the Soviet Union in the early 1990s. They may have been worth a lot once, but you could probably buy more stuff with Monopoly money now."

"Jim isn't rich?" Joe frowned at Comrade Lenin.

"Not unless the burn marks on the bills came from a time machine and he's on his way back to the USSR."

Joe asked the million-ruble question. "So what is he doing, wandering around the woods with a bundle of worthless money from a place that doesn't even exist anymore?"

"I don't know," I said as Jim began to stir. "But something smells fishy, and it isn't the tuna."

"Ugh, Frank? Joe?" Jim said groggily as he lifted himself off the ground. "Boy, is it good to see you guys. I had this awful dream that I ran into a bear."

"Did you dream about finding a stack of rubles, too?" Joe held up the money.

"Huh?" Jim rubbed his noggin and blinked away the

fuzzies. As soon as he had his focus back, he suddenly turned two shades pinker. "Oh, that. I, um, it's just, uh, well, you see—"

"What we see is our teacher in the middle of the woods with a bundle of old foreign money," Joe said before Jim could ramble on anymore. "What we'd like to know is why."

"I was going to give it back, I swear!" Jim blurted guiltily. "But then I got lost and—"

"Give it back to who?" I cut in.

"Max," he said as Joe and I looked at each other in befuddlement. "I took a stroll before bed last night to stargaze. It was only when I opened my bag to take out my telescope and found the money instead that I realized she must have taken mine when she left. You know, because our backpacks look so much alike." He looked sheepish. "I meant to bring it right back, but, well, I kind of misread my compass. I've been wandering around the woods like a doofus ever since. I guess I'm not much of a woodsman."

Jim looked at his feet in embarrassment as we tried to make sense of the story he'd just told us.

"So you weren't abducted?" I asked.

"Abducted? Whatever gave you that idea?" Jim looked perplexed. "The only thing to blame for me going missing is my own backward sense of direction."

"But what about the blood we found in your tent?" Joe wanted to know.

Jim laughed self-consciously and held up a bandaged finger.

"I kind of got my finger caught in the zipper. I feel terrible if my clumsiness scared everybody. I so badly wanted everyone to have a great trip, and here I've gone and ruined it."

Joe turned to me, looking every bit as baffled as I was. "So if he wasn't abducted, then who—"

"So wait," Jim cut in, nervously eyeing the bundle of rubles still in Joe's hand. "If I didn't imagine the whole thing about finding the money, does that mean the bear wasn't a dream either?"

"Nope." Joe pointed to giant paw prints in the mud, causing Jim to blanch. "And you didn't dream about it raiding our camp last night either."

"You mean that beast was in our camp?" he gasped, clutching the soaking-wet, torn rucksack to his chest like it was a kid's blankie.

I wanted to trust him, but I was having trouble piecing together what had happened to us the night before and how Jim wandering off with Max's bag fit into it. I looked from the "accidentally" taken money back to Jim. I was starting to get a sneaking suspicion about someone else who might have had a reason to lure that bear into camp.

"Did you find anything else in Max's rucksack with the rubles?" I asked.

"N-nothing exciting, really, just some regular gear, you know?" Jim started to turn pink again and gripped the bag even tighter. "I didn't mean to take it, though, the stuff in the bag. Which was just stuff and nothing important, really."

Jim chuckled nervously.

Joe eyed him skeptically. "If you didn't do anything wrong, then how come you're acting so shady?"

"Shady? I'm not shady! Why do you think I'm shady?" he blurted shadily, his words running together in a nervous jumble.

"Then you don't mind if we take a look?" I asked.

Jim looked genuinely hurt. "Don't you guys trust me?"

"We really, really want to, Jim," I said. "But we're going to need your help."

Jim stared at his feet and handed over the bag without meeting our eyes. "I'm sorry if I let you guys down."

Sunlight began to peek through the rain clouds, giving me a good view inside the tattered rucksack. At the very bottom, under a water bottle and some rope, was a ratty leather pouch. A sparkle of light escaped as I opened the drawstring and pulled out a gleaming green gemstone.

"Whoa!" Joe exclaimed.

But green was only the beginning. The clouds parted as I held it up and rays of sunshine burst into the forest, hitting the stone and sending a brilliant rainbow of colors sparkling over us.

"Is that . . . ?" I started to ask, but I was too stunned by the light display refracting through the gemstone to get out a complete sentence.

"Yup." Jim nodded. "It's an uncut demantoid green garnet."

"I used to dream of finding one of these when I collected

rocks as a kid," I said in awe. "It's one of the rarest precious gems in the world! But what's it doing here? I thought the good ones were found almost exclusively in only one part of Russia." I looked through the pouch and found two other demantoids, though neither one as big.

"I have no idea," Jim replied. "But I doubt anyone has discovered one that big in nearly a century. There might only be a few in the entire world!"

"That money you found may not be worth much, but I bet this sure is," Joe said, dropping the stack of rubles and holding the green stone up to the light.

I looked from the Russian money to the Russian gemstone, and it hit me. There was another notable foreign import to Black Bear Mountain that might connect the two.

"What if that Russian mobster's plane was carrying more than just the Russian mobster when it crashed thirty years ago?" I asked.

11

IT'S A TRAP

JOE

COULDN'T STOP MARVELING AT THE GEM AND the way it put on a zillion-color light show when the sun's rays hit it just right. It felt like holding a Ping-Pong-ball-size magic disco ball in the palm of my hand!

"I wonder if this is the important 'work' Max tried to cancel our trip for," I said. "Do you think she was so anxious to get rid of us because she'd stumbled on a treasure left over from the wreckage during her research?"

"Makes sense." Frank nodded. "How else would she end up coming across a stack of burned Soviet-era bills and rare Russian demantoids on Black Bear Mountain? I'm guessing that gangster's ill-gotten gains crashed along with him aboard that plane."

"A crash like that could have scattered debris over the

entire mountain," I said. "Investigators never would have been able to find every piece of the wreckage, especially not in rugged terrain like this."

"It would have been like searching for a gemstone in a haystack," Frank agreed. "That stuff could have ended up under a rock somewhere and no one would have even known it was missing."

"Or maybe someone did know," I said, eyeing our gem-stealing science teacher. "I know you said you picked up Max's bag by accident, but how do we know you didn't have a sparkling green ulterior motive for choosing this place for our camping trip to begin with?"

Jim stepped back like he'd been slapped. "What? No! I had no idea what was in it. How would I?"

"We're not saying you did, but you were the one who coordinated the trip with Dr. Kroopnik, and you did insist on us coming here even though you're terrified of flying," Frank reminded him. "Even when the rest of us thought about leaving last night, you still wouldn't hear of it."

"He could have lured the bear into camp to create a distraction, staging his own abduction so he could steal the jewel for himself," I suggested to Frank. I didn't like painting one of my favorite teachers as a villain, but his disappearance with the demantoid raised a lot more questions than he had answers.

"Joe, Frank, you have to believe me," Jim pleaded. "I didn't mean to steal it, I swear! Dr. Kroopnik took my bag and then I got lost. I didn't even know a bear came into camp last night. I would never do anything to hurt my students!"

"We want to believe you, but if you didn't mean to do it, why did you lie to us about finding the demantoids?" A hurt tone from our teacher's possible betrayal crept into Frank's voice. "Why not just tell us?"

Jim took a deep breath. "The truth is, I didn't tell you because I knew you wouldn't let me keep them and sell them."

Well, that was certainly a lot more honest than we were expecting. He must have realized how bad it sounded, because he scrambled to explain.

"I was going to do it for the Geccos. You guys know how little funding our club gets from the school. If it weren't for the generosity of Randall's parents, we never could have afforded this trip. Think of how many other great ecological expeditions we could go on with the money from those gemstones! All the good we could to do to help the environment!"

In a backward way, his logic kind of made sense. If he was telling the truth, those gems really could make a huge difference to our education as well as GECC's conservation mission. His idea had a flaw, though.

"Only they don't belong to you to sell," I said.

"They aren't Kroopnik's, either," he rationalized. "If she stole them from the crash site, then she's just as much a thief as I am.

Worse, even. A man died in that crash—she's practically a grave robber! At least I was going to do something good with them."

Jim pouted, kicking stubbornly at the dirt with his foot. "And besides, she owes us for ditching us after we went so far out of our way see her. What kind of person crushes the hopes and dreams of a bunch of kids like that? She doesn't deserve something as special as those demantoids."

It sounded like the kids weren't the only ones feeling let down by Max. Not only had Jim looked up to her as a scientist, but from the way he'd gotten all tongue-tied when Max unexpectedly rode into our lives yesterday, I think he might have had a crush on her as well. Because Jim was our teacher, it could be easy to forget he was really only a few years older than us. He was kind of almost a kid himself when you thought about it, and just then, with his broken-hearted puppy-dog pout, he looked like one too.

"Assuming you are telling the truth, what did you plan to do with the demantoids when you made it back to camp?" Frank asked. "Max has probably noticed she has the wrong backpack."

"I hadn't really figured that part out yet," he admitted. "I thought about just hiding the gemstones somewhere, but with my sense of direction, I'd probably never find it again. I guess I'm not much of an outdoorsman *or* a criminal."

"Speaking of never finding things again," I interjected, "we have to figure out a way back. The rest of the Geccos are still all by themselves at camp, and none of us are safe until we find a way off this mountain."

"Right, we can discuss this later," Frank agreed, his guard shooting back up as he scanned the woods for signs of movement. "We've wasted too much time already. Let's try to find that research station before he finds us."

I carefully placed the giant demantoid in its pouch with the others, stowed it back in the rucksack along with the rubles, and followed Frank as he crept away from the cave toward the brook.

"Hold on a second," Jim called from behind us. "Before who finds you?"

"Dude, where have you been?" I asked him. "The Mad Hermit."

"The Mad Hermit?" Jim scoffed. "Don't tell me you guys still believe Max's silly story."

Frank and I looked at each other. Thankfully, Jim hadn't been kidnapped like we thought, but that meant he didn't know what we knew about the Mad Hermit of Black Bear Mountain.

"He's real," I said. "We saw him."

"You can't be serious," he said.

"Deadly," Frank said. "We were lucky to escape with our lives."

Jim must have realized we weren't joking, because he started scurrying after us, peering over his shoulder as he went.

"If you're trying to find the research station, I know where it is," he volunteered.

"No offense, Jim, but with your backward sense of direction, I think we're better off just following Frank," I said.

"No, I saw it! I spotted it while trying to find my way back to camp. I was heading for it when I smelled someone cooking fish."

"*Bon appétit,*" I said, handing him the can of tuna, which I'd inadvertently crammed in my pocket after blowing it out when the bear showed up. "Now lead the way."

"It should be just over that ridge." He pointed uphill from the brook.

Amazingly, Jim was right. When we crested the hill, the station popped into view just a couple hundred yards away, atop the next ridge. The square cabin hovered on the edge of the ravine on a one-story-high set of stilts, giving it a 360-degree view of the entire valley from its wraparound porch. For a forest ranger, it would have made the perfect lookout for fires and poachers. We were just hoping it would make the perfect place to radio for help. We couldn't see the rapids, but we were close enough to hear them rushing down the mountain through the ravine below.

"I'll take the lead," I said. "There isn't a lot of cover once we get past that next grove of spruce trees, so just try to stay low and follow me."

We were about halfway there when Jim shrieked like he'd been launched out of a cannon. I spun around to run to defend him, only he wasn't standing behind me anymore. He was dangling upside down from a tree!

MAXED OUT 12

FRANK

TWANG! WHOOSH! AIEEEEEE!

The sound of the trip wire reached me a split second before the snare whisked Jim off the ground by his ankle.

We'd been so busy looking *up* for threats, it hadn't occurred to us that the hermit might be hunting for his meals from below!

"He's got me! He's got me!" Jim screamed.

"It's okay, Jim. It's just a tree that has you, not the hermit," Joe assured our upside-down teacher. "Hang tight and we'll have you down in a minute."

"I'm hanging tight, all right!" Jim whined.

Cutting him down wasn't a problem. Getting him to stand? Well, that was another matter.

"I think it's sprained, guys." Jim collapsed to examine his already swollen ankle. "I can't put any pressure on it. You guys are going to have to radio for help and then come back to get me."

"We're not leaving you behind," Joe declared.

"Thanks, Joe. I'm not so keen on being out here by myself either, but it would take forever to carry me all the way up that hill. The most important thing right now is getting you and the rest of the Geccos back to safety as quickly as we can."

"He's right," I said. "His ankle is so swelled up, it's turning into a cankle. Even if we were able to fashion crutches for him, he might not make it. At least here in the trees we can find him some good cover until we get back."

We got to work splinting Jim's ankle and making a quick lean-to nearby where he could rest comfortably, out of sight of hungry eyes.

"I know you guys still don't trust me about just finding the demantoids, and I know I've got a lot of work to do to rebuild that trust after lying to you," Jim said while we worked. "But I've been thinking about the whole thing, and, well, what about Randall?"

"What about him?" I asked, curious to see what Jim was getting at.

"I know it may sound like I'm just trying to deflect the blame, and I feel awful possibly pointing the finger at one of my own students, but Randall is the one who gave me the idea for the trip. He said his parents would pay for our entire stay at Bear Foot Lodge if I could arrange for the Geccos to study with Dr. Kroopnik. I hope I'm wrong about this, but his family's been coming here for years, and he'd be a lot more likely to have known about the treasure than me."

"He did already know about that plane crash before Commander Gonzo told the rest of us," I pointed out. "And he was as insistent as anybody about coming here even though he can't stand nature."

"Well, the quicker we get to that station and radio for help, the sooner we'll get a chance to ask him," Joe said. He and I left Jim behind with the rest of the water and made our final push toward the research station. The sound of the rapids crashing down the side of the mountain grew louder the closer we got. Luckily, we were approaching from the rear, so we wouldn't have to traverse the rickety wooden bridge that was suspended over the rapids from the station to the other side of the ravine.

We snuck up to the cabin's stilts, gave one last look around to make sure the coast was clear, and climbed the stairs to the deck. The door to the research station stood wide open, and it wasn't to invite us in. The place had been totally ransacked. Only this time it wasn't by bears.

"Somebody broke in looking for something," I said quietly.

Practically every drawer and cabinet in the place had been dumped out. Expensive scientific instruments lay broken amid the debris, along with framed pictures of a middle-aged scientist who might have been Max's father.

"The radio!" Joe cried, running to the counter at the back of the cabin. "It's still in one piece!"

Joe had just picked up the receiver when a silhouette appeared in the station doorway. I braced myself for a second confrontation with the hermit—and breathed a big sigh of relief when Max stepped through the door instead. I didn't know if we could trust her, but she was a lot better than the crazy ax-wielding alternative!

"I'm so glad you guys are okay," she said, rushing through the doorway. "The hermit found me before I could come back for you. There's no time to explain, but you have to follow me now. He could be back for us any second!"

Max grabbed us and started pulling us toward the door.

"We have to call for help first," Joe insisted.

"I already did. There's a plane on the way," she said. "Now let's go. We don't have much time!"

She ran for the door with Joe and me right behind. Or at least I was right behind until I snagged a shoelace on a piece of equipment, yanking my hiking boot halfway off and sending me sprawling.

"Shoot! I'll be there in a second!" I called as I tried to cram my foot back into the snug high-top boot.

"Hurry!" Max yelled, dashing toward the bridge.

I'd just managed to get my shoe back on and laced up when I noticed a large, heavy-duty cabinet marked RARE

SPECIMENS. It was the only one that hadn't been ransacked, and despite the imminent danger, I couldn't resist taking a quick peek at Max's research discoveries.

My mouth dropped open as soon as I opened the door. I'd found a rare specimen indeed—the middle-aged man from the photographs, gagged and duct-taped!

I yanked the gag out of his mouth. The man coughed and gasped for breath. "Thank you. Thank you. I thought I was never going to get out of there."

"Who are you?" I asked as I cut through the duct tape. The answer was just as shocking.

"Dr. Max Kroopnik," he said. "This is my research station."

It was my turn to sputter for breath. "But—but—"

I looked from the Max Kroopnik climbing out of the cabinet to the Max Kroopnik running across the bridge with my brother.

"But if you're Dr. Kroopnik"—I pointed out the door—"then who is she?"

THE GIRL WITH THE BEAR TATTOO

THE GIRL WITH

13

JOE

JOE!"

I was already halfway across the wobbly plank bridge when I heard my brother scream my name. Unfortunately, Max heard him first.

"Watch out!" Frank shouted.

I pivoted back toward the research station, but Max already had hold of the rucksack slung over my right shoulder. With me turning one way, Max yanking the other, and the shaky suspension bridge swaying in yet another, my body did a complete one-eighty. Next thing I knew, the bag was sliding off my arm and I was teetering against the rope rail, my arms spinning as I tried to regain my balance.

I grasped for the bag, but at that point I couldn't have cared less about the gleaming demantoid gems inside it. I needed something to grab onto or I was going to fall off the bridge!

As the shoulder strap slipped away from me, I caught a glimpse of Max's wrist where her sleeve had come undone. A bear paw with a squiggly line running through it seemed to be waving good-bye to me from the skin on her forearm.

Right before I went sailing over the rail, it occurred to me that I'd seen another arm with the same tattoo just the day before. On Casey—her sister.

Unfortunately, the family crest on Max's arm was the last thing I saw before I started plummeting toward the rapids below.

A BRIDGE TOO HIGH

14

FRANK

WATCHED HELPLESSLY AS "MAX"—OR WHO-
ever she was—snatched the rucksack from Joe's grasp,
shoving him backward in the process. The rope rail
bent beneath his weight, and for a terrifying second he
seemed to hover in the air before gravity took hold and
flipped him over the side, his body twisting as he fell.

The fall was too high, the rocks below too sharp, the
rapids too fast. There was no way he was going to survive,
unless . . .

"Yes!" I screamed as Joe grabbed hold of the bottom rope
just before it slipped from his grasp. The bridge swung vio-
lently, nearly bucking him, but he held on.

The victory didn't last long.

He only managed to pull himself halfway up before the

bridge started to come apart around him. Wood planks flew off and rained down toward the churning rapids as the ropes holding them in place began to snap. Suddenly there wasn't anything left for Joe to pull himself back onto because there was a huge gap between the remaining planks on either side of him—the rope Joe clung to had transformed from a support rail into a high wire!

He tried walking his hands back along the swaying rope, but that just caused more planks to fly free and the rope to bow dangerously, dangling Joe even lower over the rapids. I had no idea how I was going to pull him to safety, I just knew I had to try.

I leaped for the door. "Hang on, Joe! I'm coming!"

I made it only a few feet before another figure appeared in the cabin door in front of me, his hulking silhouette nearly filling the frame. There was no mistaking this person's identity; the huge ax was a dead giveaway.

With buckskin clothing that strained against his bulging muscles, a wild beard, and even wilder eyes, the Mad Hermit of Black Bear Mountain was somehow more horrifying up close than he'd been galloping at us from across the woods.

I pivoted in the opposite direction, hoping Dr. Kroopnik—the one I'd just freed, not the "Mystery Max" who'd pushed my brother off a bridge—had easy access to something we could fight the hermit off with. But the scientist apparently had other plans, because he was already halfway down a hatch in the floor at the back of the cabin.

"Follow me!" he yelled. "We can save your friend, but we have to move fast!"

I dashed after him without a second glance at the monster in the doorway.

"Stop!" the Mad Hermit bellowed after me. "I am—"

I wasn't about to wait around to hear what he had to say. I had the hatch door shut and was sliding down a rope after Dr. Kroopnik before the hermit got out another word. The rope-and-pulley system rigged for hoisting supplies up to the station made for a quick escape. I expected the hermit to be right on our tail, but when I looked behind me, he was nowhere to be seen.

I sprinted after Dr. Kroopnik toward the edge of the ravine. The bridge swayed back and forth below us, with Joe dangling over the center of the chasm, desperately clinging to the rope with both hands.

"This way!" Dr. Kroopnik shouted, hurrying down a steep flight of steps leading all the way to the riverbank below.

"But the bridge is up here!" I protested.

That's when I saw the raft tethered to the bank a few yards upstream from the bridge.

"We can to try to catch him in the raft," Dr. Kroopnik said. "It may be our only chance."

I raced down after him, past more of the exotic flowers I'd seen earlier, not that I was about to stop to examine them this time. It seemed to take us forever to get to the bottom, but when I looked up, Joe was still there, fighting to keep his grip.

"Get in!" Dr. Kroopnik yelled, pulling the raft toward the bank's edge. "I'll let out enough rope to hold you under the bridge. The river swelled from the storm, so you're going to have to fight the current to get in position."

I strained to hear him over the white water hammering the rocks and smashing against the bank as it raced past. These rapids were easily twice as bad as the ones we'd rafted down yesterday. Like the entire river was boiling over as it crashed down the mountain! Serious white-water rafters have a name for these kinds of rapids: Big Water.

Taking a deep breath, I hopped in, strapped on a life preserver, and grabbed the paddle. The rapids hammered me the instant Dr. Kroopnik pushed me off, spraying me with a face full of cold white water and rocketing the raft toward the bridge. If the raft hadn't been tethered to the bank, I would have shot right past Joe. I fought the current, digging in hard with my paddle to get in position under him.

I was nearly there when I looked up and saw that I wasn't the only one closing in. The hermit was stalking across the bridge toward him. A normal person wouldn't have been able to reach Joe across the gap in the middle of the bridge where the planks had flown off, but a normal person didn't have the enormous mountain man's long arms and long ax to close the distance.

Joe looked down in panic while I fought to position the raft beneath him. When he looked back up, the hermit stood at the edge of the gap, one long arm gripping the rope rail, the other raising the ax.

The hermit didn't get a chance to hurt him, though. My brother lost his grip first. I watched from below as the rope slipped from his fingers and he began falling through the air toward me.

15 TRUST FALL

JOE

I COULD FEEL THE ROPE SLIPPING AND HAD only a second to decide which was worse: risk falling to my death or be roasted over a fire by a crazy mountain man.

I'd felt a small surge of hope when I'd looked down and seen Frank—but a rubber raft bobbing up and down in raging white water didn't exactly make for a great safety net. Could he even catch me? Or would I just capsize the raft, taking us both down to a watery grave?

I gave one last look to the deadly rapids below and the deadly hermit above. When I looked up, the hermit's ax was raised above me. I don't know if it was the sight of the weapon looming overhead that finally did it, but I lost my grip at the exact same time the hermit lowered the ax.

Two things happened as my fingertips lost contact with the rope: the Mad Hermit's words finally reached me through the din of the rapids and I noticed the leather sheath covering the ax's lethal blade.

"I am a friend!" he yelled in a thick accent. "Grab hold!"

With no time to think, I grabbed, wrapping my fingers around the axhead an instant before the sky and the rapids could claim me.

I held on with the last bit of strength in my aching hands as the powerful hermit hoisted me back up to the bridge where the planks were still intact. I lay on my back, exhausted, my last bit of energy drained. Splintery wood never felt so good! If the Mad Hermit had tricked me so he could reel me up like a fresh-caught fish to cook over the fire, there wasn't anything I'd be able to do about it.

But instead of unsheathing his ax, he set it down and offered me his giant paw of a hand.

"Is nice to meet you," the not-so-mad hermit said in a gruff accent. "My name is Aleksei."

I gawked at my new friend. I may not have been an expert on foreign accents, but between the way he spoke and the name Aleksei, I had a good idea where he was from. It looked like the demantoid garnets and the rubles weren't the only things from Russia to survive that plane crash thirty years ago. "It's nice to meet you, Mr. Orlov, sir," I managed to sputter as I shook the hand of the very-much-alive mobster.

MAN OVERBOARD

16

FRANK

JOE GRABBING THE MAD HERMIT'S AX was the last thing I saw before the tether anchoring me to the riverbank broke.

My little raft shot down the rapids like an out-of-control speedboat, nearly tossing me over the side. I looked back, expecting to see Dr. Kroopnik standing on the bank, holding the broken rope. He still had a hold on the rope, all right, only he wasn't on the bank—he was being dragged through the water behind me!

The scientist struggled to keep his head above water as the rapids threatened to take him under. I looked frantically for a place to land, but the current was too swift and the bank way too high. Dr. Kroopnik didn't even have a life vest.

I had to find a way to get him on board before he drowned or smashed against the rocks.

I dug in hard with my paddle, cutting the raft sideways across the rapids into a patch of slightly calmer water. The raft slowed, but Dr. Kroopnik didn't, and he bodysurfed right into the boat's stern—just like I'd planned! I held the raft as steady as I could, giving him a chance to pull himself aboard before we were whisked back downstream at a furious clip.

The soaked scientist clung to the raft to keep from getting tossed right back over. The second paddle had gone overboard when the raft first broke free, so the job of trying to steer the two-man raft with only one paddle fell to me.

"Thank you!" he shouted once he had his breath back. "I thought I was a goner until you pulled that slick maneuver back there to save me."

"You got it," I said, trying to veer the raft toward the bank in search of a place to land. "Now we have to go back to save my brother, Joe!"

"We can't! Not until we're out of the ravine and the water calms down. The danger of capsizing is too great!" He had to shout to be heard over the rapids. "Besides, your brother is in good hands."

"Good hands?!" I yelled, my mind flashing back to the giant ax-wielding wild man I'd seen at the research station. "You must be madder than the Mad Hermit!"

For some reason, Dr. Kroopnik seemed to find that funny. "Trust me, the Mad Hermit is one of the good guys."

He must have seen the look of complete shock on my face, because he hesitated for a second before shouting a disclaimer. "Okay, sure, he's a notorious Russian mobster who faked his own death to avoid prosecution, but he's just about the nicest Russian mobster you'll ever meet."

The pieces finally clicked into place—the plane crash, the fugitive whose body was never found, the exotic Russian gem and the old Russian money—but I still couldn't quite believe it. "So the Mad Hermit really didn't eat that Orlov guy after his plane crashed?"

"Not unless he ate and regurgitated himself," Dr. Kroopnik yelled. "That old legend about the man-eating mountain man has been around forever; Aleksei just borrowed it to scare people off so they wouldn't find out who he really was."

"So the mythical Mad Hermit of Black Bear Mountain is real and not real, all at the same time," I said. "Talk about a great disguise!"

"Worked pretty well until a few days ago. Wait a second—" Dr. Kroopnik scrutinized me. "You really didn't know the hermit was Aleksei? I assumed you must have, since you were mixed up with that woman on the bridge."

"We thought that woman was you!"

"I can't say anyone's ever mistaken me for a beautiful woman before!" he mused at top volume. "What in the world ever gave you that idea?"

"She did!" I said. "My high school conservation club came to see Max Kroopnik and she's the one who showed up to meet us!"

"You're from the Bayport High conservation group! I'd been looking forward to meeting Mr. Morgan and his students!" he exclaimed. "I would have been waiting for you myself, but I was a little tied up."

"Ha! Usually I'm the one with the bad puns," I said with a laugh. "I'm Frank, by the way."

"Frank? Frank Hardy?" he yelled back excitedly.

"How did you know?" The famous Dr. Kroopnik knew who I was?

"Your teacher sent me your commentary on my last article. I found your observations fascinating. I was hoping we'd get a chance to talk about it in greater detail."

"Me too!" In my excitement, I nearly steered us right into a boulder. I cut hard to the left, waves slapping us in the face with cold white foam and nearly knocking Dr. Kroopnik back into the river. "But maybe we'd better save that conversation for later."

"I concur," Dr. Kroopnik agreed, gripping the raft even tighter.

The river ran down the mountain so quickly, I could feel my ears popping from the drop in elevation. I paddled like crazy to keep us upright and headed straight through the big water ahead. By the time we reached a less harrowing stretch of river, my arms felt like they were about to fall off.

We were still moving pretty fast, but the danger level had dropped a category or two, giving me a chance to rest.

"Wait a second," I said, returning to the mystery at hand. "If the Max we met isn't you, then who is she?"

"I don't have a clue," Dr. Kroopnik said, squinting at something downstream. "But maybe we should ask her."

There she was! Imposter Max rode her horse out of the woods farther downriver and took off along the bank, her blond hair flowing in the wind behind her.

I paddled against the current to keep the raft on course close to the left bank, where her horse cantered at a steady pace over the rocky terrain ahead. Miss Max didn't look back once.

"I don't think she's seen us or she'd be pushing her horse a lot harder," I said. "She's got a good head start, but we should be able to keep up as long as she sticks to the river."

"Let's follow her and see where she goes, shall we?" Dr. Kroopnik suggested. "Full speed ahead, Captain Frank!"

"You got it, Dr. K," I said as the river swept us downstream. "Although I think full speed is our only option."

"Fine by me," he replied. "I've got a bone to pick with my evil twin."

"You really don't have any idea who she is?" I asked.

"I'd been hoping you could tell me," he said. "I'd never seen her before until yesterday, when I caught her snooping around my research station. Said she got lost hiking and asked to use my radio, so I invited her in and told her to make herself at home while I went back down to bring up some gear. When I got back, I saw she'd accidentally dropped an old flyer on the floor. I bent down to pick it up and saw Aleksei's picture staring back at me. He was lot younger and didn't have that crazy beard yet, but those wild eyes of his were a dead giveaway. So was the hundred-thousand-dollar reward for information leading to his capture."

"So what did you do?" I asked with my ears tuned to Dr. K's story and my eyes set on Not Dr. K's horse up ahead.

"Best I could figure, she was some kind of bounty hunter out to get my old friend. So I turned tail and ran to warn Aleksei. But it turns out my evil twin isn't just younger and prettier than me, she's a lot faster. She clobbered me with my own microscope before I made it to the door."

"No wonder she was so eager to get rid of us," I said. "She must have been pretending to be you so we wouldn't find out the truth and alert the authorities."

"Seems that way," he observed. "At least I know she didn't get Aleksei."

"So you really are friends with that guy?" I asked, unable to shake the image of the mad cannibal from my mind. I wanted to trust Dr. Kroopnik, but we'd already been burned by one Kroopnik and I wasn't about to take any chances on another.

"He's a big, burly teddy bear, really. If he was going to eat anyone, it would have been me!" He laughed. "I accidentally stumbled right through his front door about ten years ago, shortly after I'd started my research on Black Bear Mountain. You see, I'd come across the most unlikely little garden full of *Brunnera macrophylla* growing in the middle of the woods. . . ."

"The Siberian bugloss!" I exclaimed, picturing the little blue flowers I'd seen growing in the meadow.

"You saw it too! You can imagine my excitement! Well, I followed those plants right to Aleksei's cave and disrupted his afternoon nap. Talk about finding a nonnative species! Turns out he brought seeds from his birthplace in Russia's Ural Mountains on the plane with him to make his new mountain hideout feel more like home."

"And what, he just invited you in for borscht and Russian caviar?" I asked.

"Blackberry bramble tea and smoked trout, actually," he replied. "The truth is, living all by yourself on top of a mountain in the middle of nowhere can get a little lonely, and, well, we've been good friends ever since!"

Dr. Kroopnik yelled the last part. The rapids had started to pick up speed, and from the looks of the frothing maelstrom ahead, we were about to hit the biggest water we'd seen yet. The good news was, we were closing in on the phony Miss Max.

She must have sensed us behind her, because she looked over her shoulder for the first time. I couldn't read her expression, but I knew she'd seen us from the way she kicked her horse into a full gallop. The ravine wall rose steeply to her left, trapping her along the bank, so she could run, but she couldn't hide. I just had to make sure to keep left where the river branched just ahead.

"Hold on tight!" I shouted, using all my strength to steer the raft to the left so we wouldn't lose her. "Things are about to get choppy!"

Dr. K yelled something back. I couldn't quite make it out over the churning rapids, but it sounded like he just kept repeating the word "tight" a lot. I was doing a pretty impressive job of steering, so I couldn't figure out what had him suddenly looking so panicked.

I'd just managed to guide the raft left past the fork when I realized Dr. Kroopnik hadn't been yelling "tight" at all— he'd been yelling "right." As in, he wanted me to "go right!"

Because I'd just steered us to the top of a waterfall!

MAYDAY! MAYDAY!

17

JOE

WHEN I LOOKED BACK DOWN AT the river to signal to Frank, his raft was already hurtling uncontrollably down the rapids, dragging some guy behind it like a fish on a hook.

"Hurry! We must save Max!" The not-dead Russian mobster lifted me onto my feet and began running back along the bridge toward the research station.

"Max?" I said in astonishment. "Forget about Max. That's my brother down there. We have to go after him!"

"Yes, exactly, we go save Max and your brother," he agreed nonsensically.

I was pretty sure Aleksei didn't want to eat me, but that

didn't mean he wasn't still crazy, because I couldn't figure out what in the world he was talking about.

"Max Kroopnik just tried to throw me off a bridge!" I reminded him. "She's not the one who needs saving."

"What are you talking about? Max didn't try to kill you. Strange jewel thief lady tried to kill you. And why did you call him her?" Aleksei turned back to me with a puzzled expression. "I think you hit your head when you fell. It is okay, there is a medicine kit in the helicopter. Now come on before their boat goes too far down the river!"

He took off running like a . . . well, like a madman. Aleksei sure seemed to think the guy getting dragged down the river was Max, which meant one of two things: either there were two Max Kroopniks—or our Max was an imposter. The details were going to have to wait, though.

"Back up a second," I called, running after him. "Did you say helicopter?"

"Quickest way downriver, I'll show you," he answered without breaking stride.

On the other side of the hill sat a small two-seat helicopter. Aleksei squeezed his large frame through the door and beckoned for me to join him.

"It is the chopper Max uses to fly in supplies to the mountain," Aleksei explained, punching a series of buttons as the copter whirred to life.

"Are you sure you know how to fly this thing?" I asked, reluctantly climbing into the passenger seat.

"Don't worry, I fly helicopters and planes all the time when I was a young man," he replied confidently as he examined the controls. "Now, where is the button that makes it go up?"

I groaned. "Yeah, but wasn't that, like, thirty years ago?"

I was starting to have serious reservations about boarding an aircraft with a crazy-looking Russian mountain man who hadn't flown anything in three decades and crashed the last plane he *had* flown!

"Flying is like riding bike. You don't forget," he assured me. "Besides, I never crash anything I don't mean to."

Somehow, that didn't make me feel any better, not that I had time for second thoughts about our mode of transportation. We were airborne! Sort of . . .

The small chopper hovered unsteadily, dipping and diving as Aleksei tried to figure out the controls. And I'd thought flying with Commander Gonzo was scary!

The chopper's two-way radio took my mind off our possible impending doom. I tried tuning it to the emergency channel, but there was too much static to tell if anyone was on the other end.

"MAYDAY! MAYDAY!" I shouted into the radio. "There's a man overboard in the rapids below the old ranger lookout station on Black Bear Mountain, and four campers are stranded nearby, one of them injured. Please send help."

I repeated the message two more times before hanging up, hoping my pleas for help had reached someone—and hoping they wouldn't have to rescue the two guys in the helicopter as well. Aleksei was still trying to get control over the copter, which was bobbing and weaving like a punch-drunk bumblebee as he tried to keep it over the river so we could look for Frank's raft.

"So you must be the young science students Max was so excited to meet," he said after hearing my Mayday call. "I am sorry. It is my fault the jewel thief lady ruined the trip for everybody and put you in danger."

It sounded like Aleksei's Max was the real Max after all. I also had a hunch that Dr. Kroopnik wasn't the only one she'd impersonated. Frank and I hadn't been able to see the rider's features from across the clearing beneath the crazy mountain man getup, but . . .

"That wasn't you who tried to run us down while we were lighting the signal fire, was it?"

"Why would I want to run you down? I just met you," came Aleksei's perplexed reply.

"So you don't know who that woman is either?" I asked.

"No, this party-pooper lady is a mystery to me. Nobody in the world knows I am here except Max Kroopnik." He paused to growl in my direction. "And now you."

I gulped. I couldn't tell whether he meant it as an observation or a threat. "I'd never heard of Aleksei Orlov or the Mad Hermit until yesterday! My brother and I are just good at solving mysteries, and I was able to put the clues together."

He pondered my explanation for a minute before nodding. "Yes, I didn't think you were my adversary. I think this woman hoodwinked you, too," he said. "Maybe young detective and Aleksei can solve mystery together, eh?"

I mulled over the evidence in my head, trying to figure out how Jim or Randall might still fit into it. One clue had my mind racing more than the others, though. "Well, she does have the same family tattoo on her arm as Casey—Casey is the woman who owns the Bear Foot Lodge, where we were staying before we came up here—so I'm pretty sure they're sisters and she's mixed up in this too," I shared. "Frank overheard someone arguing about us being in danger before we left, and I bet it was Casey on the radio with the perp. But why would she want to pose as Dr. Kroopnik anyway?"

"I do not know this barefoot place or why she pretend to you to be Dr. Max," he said. "Is very troubling. How this woman found me, I do not know, but she stole my stash of precious Russian gems."

"So the demantoids are yours," I said. "There were a few in her rucksack. My brother Frank and I figured they came from your plane wreck; we just never guessed you were still alive to enjoy them!"

"Yes, she took others as well," he said. "She raided my secret hiding place, and the ones in Max's cabin are gone also."

"Um, no offense, but why would a field biologist be

stashing a mobster's jewels?" my brain asked before my mouth had a chance to censor it. Aleksei didn't seem to take offense, though.

"Max is a good friend. He helps me by taking them into the city to sell."

"Dr. Kroopnik is helping you sell stolen jewels?" I blurted, again without thinking.

"I have stolen many things in my life, but not jewels. The demantoids are mine from Russia," he explained without getting angry (though it was kind of hard to tell with that gruff accent of his). "Max is a good man. He sells the stones to donate money to charity in the name of the innocent victims of my old crimes. He helps me do a good thing to maybe make amends for some of the ugly things I did in my previous life of crime."

As long as I was blurting out offensive questions, I figured I might as well go for broke. "Uh, like what kind of ugly things?"

He tugged on his beard ruefully.

"I did many financial scams and took much money that was not mine," he admitted. "But I never caused anybody to be hurt by violence. Still, I know now that it is wrong, but I could not go to prison. I would miss the sunshine of my beautiful gardens too much. So I find a beautiful remote place to disappear. I even had my little toe cut off by a doctor friend to leave in crashed plane so they will find evidence I am dead and not look for me! Is very clever, no?"

"Now, that's dedication, dude," I said, marveling at how much of the campfire tale about the Mad Hermit of Black Bear Mountain was actually true. The investigators really had found a toe—it just hadn't been gnawed on by a cannibal!

"I planned to wait for the police and prosecutor to forget about Aleksei, and then go home to my old life, but I like it so much on my mountain, I stay!" he declared. "All the wealth I need is right here in nature."

Aleksei seemed to have the hang of the controls by now and had the little helicopter zipping along above the river.

"The rapids are fast, but we are faster," he said. "Keep a lookout for the raft."

Listening to Aleksei's story had distracted me from thinking about Frank and Dr. Kroopnik getting sucked down the gnarliest stretch of rapids I'd ever seen. The rapids had tapered off for a while, which had given me hope that Frank might have been able to steer the raft ashore, but there'd been no sign of the red raft anywhere. And now the rapids were picking up again. And I mean picking up. From above, the river looked like a boiling cauldron filled with jagged rocks.

My heart sank when I saw the waterfall. It sank further when I saw the flash of red at the bottom.

"No!" I screamed, pressing my face to the glass, searching for signs of life near Frank's torn and tattered raft.

HIGH DIVE 18

FRANK

B Y THE TIME I SAW THE WATERFALL, IT was already too late to do anything about it. The current grabbed ahold of the raft and slung us over the edge before I could even scream.

It may not have been the most scientific experiment, but I think Dr. Kroopnik and I proved conclusively that rafts aren't meant to fly. The rubber raft went one way and Dr. K and I each went another. Forty horrifying feet later, I splashed feetfirst into a vat of white water.

Luckily, the pool at the bottom of the falls was deep enough that I didn't smash against the rocks, and the water spat me out again in one piece. My life vest kept me afloat as the current swept me farther downstream. As soon as I spotted a small break in the rapids, I swam as hard as I could for the bank and grabbed onto a fallen branch before the river could suck me back in.

I collapsed onto dry ground, coughing water and trying to catch my breath as I searched the river for Dr. Kroopnik. Shredded rubber was all that remained of the raft, but luckily, Dr. K was in better shape. He was doing the same thing as me, farther upstream on the opposite bank.

We waved to each other to signal we were okay, but that was about all the communicating we could achieve across a river full of thundering rapids. Looking around to get my bearings, I spotted the horse's tracks along the bank. Not that it did me much good. "Don't Call Me Maxine" was long gone, and it wasn't like I could catch up on foot.

Stranded again! Or maybe not. I looked back upstream at the waterfall—the viewing angle was new, but the setting wasn't. I'd seen the same waterfall in the distance while zipping across the river back to the lodge the day before!

Which meant I had a pretty good idea how to find the cliff ledge with the zip line launch back to the lodge. I signaled to Dr. K to keep heading downstream, gave him a thumbs-up to let him know I had a plan, and took off running through the woods, using my memory of the topography from the zip line to guide me.

It didn't really hit me until I reached the zip line that I'd actually have to ride the dreadful thing again if I wanted to make it back to the lodge. It had been terrifying enough while safely strapped in with a helmet on and a professional there to make sure everything went smoothly. This time I'd be on my own, rocketing across the valley at fifty miles per hour without even a harness to stop me from falling.

Fear gripped my gut as I stood there looking at the vastness below. I had to step back from the ledge. I couldn't go through with it.

But then an image of Joe dangling from the bridge flashed into my head . . . and our teacher, Jim, alone and hurt on Black Bear Mountain . . . and the rest of the Geccos, Melissa and Mandy and even Randall, still stranded at camp, fearing for their lives.

I grabbed hold of the handlebar and leaped off the cliff before I had a chance to second-guess myself. I gripped the bar so tightly I thought the metal might bend, and I screamed like a madman as the river sped closer. The lodge came into view on the other side, and for a second I thought I might actually make it. But then something else came into view as well—the blond Max imposter racing her horse along the riverbank upstream from the lodge.

The horse heard me before "Max" saw me. The poor animal spooked at the sound of me hurtling toward it and reared up, catching its rider off guard and bucking her into the river along with her rucksack.

The water was a lot calmer there by the lodge, but from the way she was splashing around frantically, you'd have thought she'd been the one tossed off a waterfall. I was just about to zip right over her when I realized why—she couldn't swim!

She was a fraud and a thief and she'd put all our lives in danger, but it was our job to catch criminals, not punish them. I couldn't just watch another person drown.

I leaped from the zip line without thinking about it. Which, I quickly realized while plummeting toward the river for the second time in less than an hour, may not have been the smartest idea ever.

CATCH OF THE DAY

19

JOE

"I DON'T SEE THEM!" I CRIED, HOPING THAT meant Frank and the real Max had somehow survived the waterfall. "We have to go down there and look!"

"We can't. There is nowhere to land the chopper," Aleksei said. "We must search from the air. They may have washed . . ."

The big Russian stopped in midsentence, but I already knew what he'd been thinking—if they didn't make it, we might find their bodies washed up downstream. I shoved the thought from my mind and kept searching the riverbank below.

I was so focused on the river, I almost didn't notice the valley opening up on either side.

"This is closest to the outside world I have been in thirty

years," Aleksei reflected softly as the helicopter followed the river through the winding valley.

When I looked up from the water, I saw cabins and a small country road off to the right. We were still surrounded by beautiful mountains, but there were also signs of civilization—and I recognized them!

"Keep following the river!" I shouted. "We're not far from the lodge! We can get help there! They might even have made it back!"

The mobster-turned-hermit mumbled something to himself, his brow furrowed deep in thought. It suddenly struck me that I hadn't merely asked Aleksei to fly me back to the lodge. I'd asked him to risk blowing the cover he'd gone to such great lengths to protect—and maybe even go to prison for it.

"Aleksei, I know this is a lot to ask, but my brother . . ."

"Shhh," he commanded, gripping my shoulder firmly. "I know what you are going to say."

My whole body tensed. Who had I been kidding? There was no way the fugitive was going to take me to the lodge. It wasn't like he could just drop me off without anyone noticing a giant mountain man landing a helicopter in the backyard. What was I supposed to say when he left—that I called for a chopper? Even if I could somehow leave him out of it, Black Bear Mountain was going to be crawling with search teams as soon as I told everyone what had happened to Frank and the Geccos. Either way, taking me back to the lodge meant the possibility of Aleksei getting caught. If

Aleksei decided to turn the chopper around and save himself, there was nothing I could do. I didn't stand a chance against the big hermit, and I couldn't fly a helicopter myself even if I did. Aleksei's grip on my shoulder tightened.

"It is to great lengths I went to make Aleksei Orlov disappear. Nearly twice as long as you have been alive I have spent keeping my identity a secret," he rumbled "I have had much time to think. I did many bad things in my old life, but I am a different man now, and I do not want to give up my freedom."

He paused, and my gut sank.

"But Max is my friend, and you too are now my friend," he continued somberly. "I cannot allow more people to be hurt because of me. For Max and your brother, I will take you back. I will stay by your side until they are safe, even if it means I never get to see my beautiful mountain again."

"Thank you, Aleksei!" I cheered. "That's a really heroic thing for you to do."

"Hmm." He grinned. "The Heroic Hermit of Black Bear Mountain. I like!"

Bear Foot Lodge came into view around the next bend. With horses grazing serenely in the pasture and Chief Olaf wading into the river to reel in a big fish, it looked like a picture straight out of a travel brochure. You'd never know it was the source of so much danger.

"There it is!" I said. "Can you put us down in the field behind the lodge?"

The propeller blast from the chopper pounded the river's surface with wind, sending Chief Olaf's fish flying off his hook. I had a feeling I was a lot happier to see the chief than he was going to be to see me.

The soaking-wet chief stomped up, holding his fish-less line, as Aleksei landed the helicopter behind the lodge. "What in the world is going on here? Do you have any idea how long it took me to land that trout? I—" Then he saw me. "Joe? I should have figured . . ."

"Have you seen Frank?" I leaped out of the chopper, cutting him off.

He looked at me like I was nuts. "Why would I have seen Frank? I thought you boys were supposed to be camping up on Black Bear Mountain."

"Something terrible has happened," I explained. "We have to get a search team upriver now! Frank's raft went over the falls, Jim is hurt, and the rest of us are still stranded on the mountain!"

The chief's annoyance instantly turned to concern. "Slow down, son, and tell me exactly what happened."

"I'm still trying to put the pieces together, Chief, but—"

A female voice cut in before I could finish.

"What is that helicopter doing on my property?" Casey came running out of the lodge, sleeves rolled up, exposing the bear-paw tattoo on her forearm. "Joe? What are you doing here? Who is this guy?"

She looked up at Aleksei, towering silently by my side.

"As if you don't know," I spat before turning to Chief Olaf.

The chief looked just as stunned as Casey. "Her sister impersonated Dr. Kroopnik to deceive us as part of a conspiracy to commit theft," I informed the chief. "And my brother and Dr. Kroopnik are still missing or maybe even worse because of it."

"M-my sister?" Casey stammered. "Is this some kind of joke? I haven't seen Lana in weeks."

"I saw your family crest tattooed on her arm right before she pushed me off a bridge," I seethed.

Casey's jaw dropped, and she reflexively rubbed at the bear paw on her forearm. "But that's crazy! Lana's off camping somewhere out west. She isn't even in the state!"

"Let's slow down a second, Joe." Chief Olaf put a hand on my shoulder to calm me down. "Now, I've known you long enough to know you're being straight with me, but let's not be hasty. I'm out of my jurisdiction up here, but even if I wasn't, we need to gather more facts and make sure we're not just jumping to conclusions. And if you're right, I'll do what I can to step in until the local authorities get here."

I took a deep breath and nodded. Seeing Frank's raft torn up like that had my emotions running high, and I'd let my heart do the detecting instead of my brain.

"You're right, Chief," I conceded. "A good detective stays objective and doesn't rush to judgment, but I know for a fact that the woman responsible for this has an identical tattoo on her right arm."

"I swear I don't know what you're talking about," Casey pleaded. "My sister wouldn't want to hurt any of my guests. She knows how much the lodge means to me. Are you sure it wasn't a different tattoo? All kinds of people have tattoos up here."

"Bear paws with squiggly lines down the center that match the path of the river through the valley?" I asked.

"Oh," she said meekly. "But I don't understand."

Either Casey was a great liar or she was genuinely clueless about my accusation.

"When was the last time you saw her?" I asked, wondering if the Geccos hadn't been the only ones duped by her sister.

"Maybe two, three weeks ago," Casey said. "She's always off on some outdoor adventure somewhere or another. She was supposed to stop by the lodge for a visit after her last trip up Black Bear Mountain, but she called at the last minute to cancel. She said she found this great expedition she wanted to go on with some famous mountain man or something. I don't know why she would have lied to me."

One of the things you learn in detective work is that sometimes the most believable lies also contain a bit of truth, and I had a pretty good idea which "famous mountain man" Casey's sister had been talking about. I glanced back at Aleksei, who had retreated to the helicopter in an attempt to eavesdrop without drawing attention to himself—and for a giant hermit with a woolly beard and buckskins, he was doing a pretty good job. Casey seemed to have forgotten about him and the helicopter altogether. If she knew who he was, it sure didn't show.

She seemed totally bewildered and blindsided by everything I'd said. I thought about how cool of a host she'd been the day before and found myself wanting to believe she'd been conned by her sister along with the rest of us. But Frank had overheard someone at the lodge arguing on the radio about the crazy hermit in the woods before we left, and if it wasn't Casey, then who?

Chief Olaf continued to question Casey, but I was already searching for answers somewhere else. I rewound my memory to the day before. We'd been standing behind the lodge in pretty much the same place, getting ready to go meet Dr. Kroopnik, when Jim had freaked out about flying with Commander Gonzo—and the person who kept trying to talk us out of going to Black Bear Mountain hadn't been Casey. It had been her husband.

"Where is Steven?" I asked, interrupting the chief.

"Steven?" she repeated. "I . . . I'm not sure. He got a call on the radio earlier and said he had to go upstream to check on the fence in the north pasture, but he should have been back by now. Why do you . . . ?"

The sound of someone screaming like their hair was on fire reached us from upriver before she could finish. I knew that voice! I'd heard the same distressed cry yesterday after I'd talked my brother into riding the zip line.

"Frank!" I yelled, and took off running for the riverbank with Chief Olaf, Casey, and Aleksei right behind me.

A riderless horse stood on the bank farther upstream, watching as Frank struggled to pull Dr. Kroopnik's thrashing imposter to shore. My brother and I both had lifeguard training, but a panicking drowning victim can drag even a strong swimmer down with them.

"Lana?!" Casey gasped. "She never learned to swim! She's terrified of water!"

All four of us sprinted for the water's edge. Before we could reach it, we realized Frank and Lana weren't the only ones in the river. Steven was already swimming toward them.

RESOLUTION RIVER

20

FRANK

LEAPING OFF THE ZIP LINE INTO THE river turned out to be the easy part. I'd jumped in to save her on impulse, and it wasn't until I splashed down beside the flailing mystery woman that I remembered one of the basic rules of lifeguarding—don't let one drowning become two! You only approach a drowning swimmer in open water as a last resort, because of the risk that they'll unintentionally take you under. Which is exactly what was happening!

I tried to swim ahead of her so I could pull her back to shore, but she wouldn't stop trying to climb on top of me in a desperate attempt to escape the river. Even with my life vest still on, I had to fight to keep my head above water as she struggled. I wanted to tell her I was trying to help, but it's hard to talk with a mouth full of river water.

I'd started to think we both might wind up as fish food when I saw a pair of long, skinny arms and a beard slicing through the water toward us. Steven! I was so happy for the help, I didn't stop to think what he was doing there. Max's imposter actually calmed down a little when she saw Steven, and together we were able to swim her back to the shallows.

What I hadn't been expecting was a welcoming committee waiting for us on the riverbank! Seeing Joe next to Aleksei "Mad Hermit" Orlov and Chief Olaf in his fishing getup had to be one of the most welcome, not to mention strangest, sights of my life.

I gave Joe a big, soggy bear hug. "Man, is it good to see you!"

"Likewise, bro," he replied with a grin. "You've spent so much time in the water today, I think you're starting to sprout gills."

"You are Frank, yes?" the big hermit asked. "You have seen my friend Max? He is okay?"

"He's okay," I assured him. "We wiped out on opposite sides of the river and he's got a long hike ahead of him, but he isn't hurt."

"What about Jim?" Chief Olaf asked. "You said he was hurt?"

"He sprained his ankle pretty badly, but we splinted him

up and left him resting near the old ranger station with some water," Joe said. "He should be okay for a while at least."

Steven carried Maxine, or whoever she was, the rest of the way onto the bank, where she crumpled to the ground, coughing water and gasping for breath.

Casey immediately ran to her side. "Lana! Oh my God, are you okay?"

I was about to ask how Casey knew our mystery woman when I saw the matching bear-paw tattoos on both their arms. "'Don't Call Me Maxine' is Casey's sister!" I blurted out.

"And I have a hunch Steven here is who you overheard talking on the radio with her before we left for our little misadventure." Joe fixed the lanky lodge keeper with a glare.

Steven gave a panicked glance from my brother to the very mad Mad Hermit standing next to him and turned to run. The look on Casey's face stopped him in his tracks. She was a bundle of fear, surprise, and hurt all in one.

"Steven?" she said softly. "Why is Lana here? They think we've done something to hurt the Bayport High kids, but it's all just some kind of big misunderstanding, right?"

Steven looked away. "We were trying to help. No one was ever supposed to get hurt."

"Trying to help . . . ?" Casey repeated. "But I don't understand."

Unable to look his wife in the eye, Steven turned to us. "Whatever happens next, Casey didn't know anything about any of this. She never would've let Lana and me get ourselves into this mess if she had."

"Any of what?" Casey and Chief Olaf demanded at the same time.

"Kidnapping Dr. Kroopnik, stealing his identity, stranding a bunch of kids in the wilderness, and throwing Joe off a bridge, for starters," I said when neither Lana nor Steven spoke up. Lana was still on the ground, recovering from nearly drowning, but Steven had that panicked look in his eyes again like he might try to run.

Aleksei growled and Chief Olaf fixed Steven with one of his patented "bad cop" glares. "Are you going to cooperate? I'd really rather us not have to restrain you."

"Yes, sir," Steven said, the fight draining out of him. "Just so long as Casey isn't blamed for anything we did."

He looked over at Lana, who nodded meekly. Casey stumbled away from her sister like being close to either her or Steven might burn her.

"Speak for yourself next time," Aleksei said to Chief Olaf in a thick Russian accent. "I would very much like to restrain them."

"I'm sorry, but who are you again?" Chief Olaf asked, apprehensively eyeing the big, burly, bushy-bearded, buckskin-wearing mountain man.

Aleksei hesitated and looked down at Joe.

"Chief, this is my friend Aleksei," Joe said proudly. "He saved my life on the bridge."

"And he fits into this whole thing how?" the chief asked.

"Well . . . I . . . uh . . ." Aleksei cleared his throat. "You see, it's . . . uh . . . mmm . . ."

"He's Aleksei Orlov, sir," Steven explained timidly. "Lana found out he was hiding on Black Bear Mountain on her camping trip a couple of weeks ago. We wanted to get proof to take to the FBI so we could collect the reward."

"Aleksei Orlov?" The chief mulled the name over. "Wait, isn't that the name of that Russian mobster who crashed his plane up here all those years ago?"

Aleksei smiled guiltily.

"But you're supposed to be dead!" the chief exclaimed.

"If I am dead, then it is okay if I go?" Aleksei asked hopefully.

"What? No!" Chief Olaf looked from Aleksei to us. "Leave it to the Hardy boys to go camping and come back with a dead Russian mobster!"

"He faked his death." Lana spoke up for the first time, her voice hoarse from nearly drowning. "I stumbled on his hideout in a cave and saw a newspaper clipping about a reward for information leading to his capture from before the plane crash."

"She called me when she got back and I looked it up," Steven added. "They never got around to taking the reward off the books after the crash, so we thought we could still collect it if we told the police."

"Only they just laughed at us," Lana said bitterly. "Like

we'd told them about seeing a flying saucer or something."

Steven nodded. "We figured if we could get proof and show them we were telling the truth, they would have to give us the reward."

"So I went back with my camera to get his picture and maybe some kind of DNA evidence or something," Lana said.

"You what?!" Casey looked from her sister to her husband with her mouth wide open.

"We did it for you, honey," Steven said sheepishly. "I know you wanted to make Bear Foot Lodge work without having to ask anybody for help, but we were so far behind on our bills. We thought if we used the reward money to pay off all the debt, then the bank would have to leave us alone."

"Hard work is what's going to keep Bear Foot Lodge running, not some risky get-rich-quick scheme," Casey scolded.

Steven hung his head. "We didn't tell you because we knew you'd say it was too dangerous."

"Of course I'd say it's too dangerous!" she shouted. "Look at what happened!"

"But we almost did it!" Lana defended herself. "Everything was going perfectly until . . ."

"Dr. Kroopnik caught you trying to snitch on his friend, so you knocked him out, tied him up, and stuck him in a cabinet?" I added up the missing pieces for her.

Casey gasped.

"I didn't mean to," Lana squeaked. "I just kind of panicked."

The whole puzzle was starting to come together now that we had Lana and Steven talking.

"And then you radioed Steven from the research station to tell him what happened, and when he couldn't talk Jim out of taking us to Black Bear Mountain to see Max Kroopnik, you showed up in his place pretending to be Dr. 'Maxine' Kroopnik so we wouldn't know the real Max was missing," Joe said, reconstructing their plot. "Only we wouldn't leave when you canceled the field trip, so you tried to scare us off with the story about the Mad Hermit."

Aleksei growled in Lana's direction.

"Pretty clever, the way you mixed fact and fiction to really frighten us with that campfire tale, but Jim still wouldn't budge," I said, picking up where Joe left off. "So you cut down our food to lure the bear into camp, figuring a hungry black bear would scare us off for good."

I guessed at that last part, but Lana just stared down at her soggy boots, letting me know I was right about the identity of the bear's accomplice.

"But Jim messed up your plan by wandering off and getting lost, which left you stuck with a second missing person and five stranded teenagers," I speculated. I really hoped I was right, because there was still the unpleasant possibility that our teacher was mixed up in this somehow. I breathed a sigh of relief when Lana nodded.

"I guess I scared myself with that story too," she admitted. "I really thought the Mad Herm—uh, I mean Mr. Orlov—took him. Besides that, I'd somehow ended up with your teacher's backpack. So I just kind of improvised to buy myself some time until I could get my own bag back, because it had all the stuff in it."

"She radioed me from the station to meet her here by the river," Steven said. "I was waiting when her horse threw her in the water."

"Thanks, by the way, for trying to save me, Frank," Lana said sheepishly. "It was a really brave thing for you to do, especially after I ruined your trip."

"Um, thanks," I mumbled, trying not to blush. It's still nice getting compliments from a beautiful girl, even if she was a criminal who almost got you killed a few times.

"Excuse me, miss," the chief said to Lana. "But can you skip back to the part where you decided it was a good idea to throw Joe off a bridge?" Chief Olaf asked.

"I didn't mean to!" she said. "I was just trying to get the garnets back. I didn't realize he fell over the side until I looked back."

"Garnets? What garnets?" the chief and Casey asked at the exact same time.

"Excuse me, Mr. Chief," Aleksei interrupted. "You are a policeman, yes? I would like to report a robbery."

"I'm sorry, what?" Chief Olaf said, looking from Lana to Aleksei.

"This woman has stolen my personal collection of dem-antoids that I have brought with me all the way from my homeland," Aleksei accused.

"Deman-who?" the chief asked.

"Demantoid green garnets from the Ural Mountains of Russia," Aleksei explained. "They are very meaningful to me, and I would like to have them back."

Lana winced. "I don't have them. They were all in my bag when I fell in the river."

"All of them?" Aleksei asked fretfully.

She nodded. Aleksei cast a sad look at the river and then shrugged it off. "It is okay. From nature they came. Back to nature they go."

Chief Olaf looked at Joe and me and threw up his hands. "Can't you boys ever bring me a normal case?! Green gar-nets, mad hermits, and living dead Russian mobsters. The whole thing has my head spinning."

"We like to keep you on your toes, Chief," Joe said.

"So much for my fishing trip," the chief sighed, turning to Steven and Lana. "I'm going to have to take the two of you into custody until the local police can get here to sort this mess out. You're not going to give me any more trouble, are you?"

"No, sir," they both said.

"I'm so sorry, Casey . . . ," Steven started to say, but Casey had already started running back to the lodge.

"What about Aleksei, Chief?" Joe asked hopefully.

"Yes, I go home?" Aleksei asked, sounding more like a little boy than a giant hermit.

"I'm sorry, I can't let you do that, Mr. Orlov," the chief reluctantly told the giant mountain-man mobster. "I'm very grateful to you for helping Joe, and I'll put in a good word for you, but I can't let a known fugitive go just because he's a nice guy."

Aleksei let out a little moan.

"I wish I didn't have to ask you this," the chief gulped, looking up at the huge hermit. "But you're not going to resist this, are you?" He sounded a lot less confident asking Aleksei than he had Steven and Lana.

"I will not fight," Aleksei conceded. "I was a criminal once, but never a violent man."

Joe's face suddenly lit up. "That's it! You said you were charged with financial crimes, right, Aleksei? And it was thirty years ago?"

"Yes, embezzlement and money laundering were the only charges."

"I don't see what that has to do with anything, Joe," the chief said.

I did, though! I'd taken an online criminal law course from the local college, and Joe had helped me study. Different crimes don't just carry different penalties, some stay on the books for a lot less time than others.

"The statute of limitations, Chief!" I said. "They've expired! A person can only be prosecuted for certain crimes for a specific number of years after they were committed—and embezzlement and money laundering are both less than ten years!"

The chief looked at me warily and sighed one of his chief-size sighs. "I know better than to challenge Frank Hardy on a technical detail."

"Yes!" I high-fived Joe as Aleksei lifted us both off the ground in a huge hermit hug.

"The local authorities may still want to talk to you about this mess," the chief said. "But as far as I'm concerned, my jurisdiction for the rest of this trip doesn't go past the fishing hole!"

Dr. K trudged up a little while later to join the celebration. Commander Gonzo radioed a few minutes after that to say he'd gotten Joe's distress call from the chopper; he'd coordinated with the rangers and was already on his way back to the lodge with Jim and the rest of the Geccos.

"I'm sorry you lost all your demantoid garnets," Joe said to Aleksei as we sat with him and Dr. K around a campfire behind the lodge, watching Gonzo's plane come in for a landing.

"Who knows?" the hermit said with a sparkle in his eye. "Maybe there is still one more secret hiding place that jewel thief lady did not find, eh?"

"No way?!" I said.

Dr. K grinned as Aleksei twirled a strand of his unruly beard. It was hard to tell behind all that facial hair, but I'm pretty sure he was smiling.

"Maybe Miss Casey at Barefoot Lodge gets an anonymous donation to help with the bills so my young friends have a nice place to stay when they visit their old buddies Aleksei and Max."

Joe and I were still processing Aleksei's latest whopper of a surprise when Gonzo's plane rumbled to a stop.

"Frank!" Melissa yelled, hopping out of the little plane and running across the field.

"Joe!" Mandy yelled from right beside her. Jim hobbled along behind them on crutches with a big grin on his face. Even Randall was smiling.

They must not have heard about our new friend, though, because all four of them nearly fainted when they saw us sitting around the campfire, roasting marshmallows with the Heroic Hermit of Black Bear Mountain.

BOUND FOR DANGER

FRANK

HAVE YOU EVER HAD A DREAM?

A dream that was worth risking it all? Putting yourself in uncomfortable situations? Facing your fears?

I had that dream. But I'd only recently discovered it.

Three weeks ago, I joined the Bayport High B-Sharps, an a cappella singing group. That's right. *A cappella.* I know most people picture dorky guys in cardigans singing yet another goofy version of Billy Joel's "The Longest Time," but the B-Sharps aren't like that. For one thing, we don't wear cardigans. For another, our captain, Max Crandal, has a strict "no Billy Joel" policy. (It's not that we have anything against Billy Joel, personally. It's just the cliché of the thing.)

And so here I was, heart pounding in my chest, sweaty fists clenched in my pockets. I was about to make my debut with the B-Sharps, performing "The Lion Sleeps Tonight" at a freshman antibullying assembly. I wasn't totally sure what the connection was, topic-wise. All I knew was that I had a solo: "In the village, the peaceful village, the lion . . ."

"How are you doing, Frank?" Max walked up to me and patted me on the back. We were in the wings of the stage, waiting for the Bayport High Improv Group to finish up a sketch, and then we were up.

"I'm good, I'm totally good," I lied. The truth was I was *freaking out*, but I was determined to conquer my fears.

"You really killed it in rehearsal yesterday," Max said with a sincere smile. "I'm sure you'll do great."

I smiled back and thanked him. Max is a stand-up guy, a great captain. He was part of why I was enjoying my time with the B-Sharps so much.

I turned back to the sketch that was wrapping up onstage. The girl playing the person being bullied was being very open and honest about how the bullying made her feel, and the bully was talking about how problems at home were making her act out. My palms started sweating even harder. *Oh God, we're up in, like, one . . .*

"Frank Hardy?"

I turned around, surprised. I'd been so focused on the skit that I hadn't noticed someone walking up behind me. Now I looked down at Seth Diller, Bayport High's own amateur filmmaker, president of the school's AV club, and a vague acquaintance.

"Principal Gerther wants to see you," he said, flashing an official pink request form. When you got one of those, you had to report to the office immediately.

"What does Principal Gerther want?" I asked. It still felt a little weird to refer to him that way. For most of my high school career, he'd been the low-level coach who oversaw study hall. But then my brother Joe and I had found the acting principal to be involved in some pretty serious shenanigans, and Gerther was promoted.

Seth shrugged. "It's not my job to ask why," he said, waving the form. "It's my job to come and get you, okay? I'm just a messenger."

The skit was finishing up now.

"Can it wait five minutes? I have a part in the next song." I gestured around to my a cappella amigos.

Seth shook his head. "If you look at the form," he said in an annoyed tone, tapping an X on the pink paper, "it says right here, 'VERY URGENT.' That means no waiting, no bathroom breaks, no stopping at your locker. We need to go *now*."

I glanced back at Seth. "But . . ."

Max stepped forward. The skit had ended now and the improv kids were shuffling backstage. "It's all right, Frank," he said. "Whatever Gerther needs you for, it must be important. Go ahead, we can cover for you."

I sighed, hesitating. I didn't *want* to go. I wanted to kill it during my solo!

Seth waved the form at me again. "Gerther said if we're not back in ten minutes, we both get detention," he said. "I don't know what this is about, but it must be serious."

Great, I thought. "All right, all right," I said, beckoning in front of me. "Lead the way, Seth. I'm sorry, Max."

"No worries." Max shook his head like I shouldn't give it another thought. He really is the nicest guy. "I just hope it all works out."

With a wave to the others, I scurried off to follow Seth, who was already halfway down the aisle to the auditorium entrance. He didn't slow down when he saw I was following him, and I ended up practically running after him the whole way to the office.

Where I found my brother, Joe, waiting. He cocked his eyebrows in surprise when he saw me. *Hmmmm.* If Joe and I were both being called in, that narrowed down the possible topics. To one.

Joe and I aren't perfect students, but we're not the types to get urgently called into the principal's office that often either. And if Gerther wanted to talk to the two of us together, it pretty much had to be about our sleuthing hobby.

"What do you think this is about?" Joe whispered to me when I sat down in a hard plastic chair beside him. Seth dropped off the URGENT pink form with the receptionist, then disappeared into the mailroom.

"I don't know," I admitted. "We haven't worked a case in a few weeks."

Before we could theorize much further, Principal Gerther's door opened and he nodded at us, shouting, "HARDY BOYS? GOOD. COME IN, PLEASE!"

Principal Gerther lost something like 80 percent of his hearing fighting in Vietnam. He yells everything, and doesn't quite understand when people don't yell back.

Joe and I stood and wandered into his office.

"HAVE A SEAT," he barked, settling into his fancy office chair. As Joe and I sat, I noticed that Gerther had pulled out our encyclopedia-size permanent files, and they were sitting on his desk in front of him.

"SO," said Joe, smiling a friendly smile, and affecting the 50 percent volume increase necessary to communicate with our principal. "IS EVERYTHING OKAY? FRANK AND I WERE A BIT SURPRISED TO BE CALLED IN TODAY."

Principal Gerther nodded impatiently. "YES, SURE. EVERYTHING IS FINE, BOYS, BUT I'VE BEEN LOOKING OVER YOUR TRANSCRIPTS." He gestured to the huge files in front of him. "I COULDN'T HELP NOTING THAT THERE'S A LACK OF EXTRACURRICULAR ACTIVITIES."

I looked at Joe in surprise. *What?*

Coach Gerther pointed a chubby finger at us. "YOU'RE GOING TO BE APPLYING TO COLLEGE SOON," he said, "OR AT LEAST FRANK WILL. YOU MUST KNOW HOW COMPETITIVE IT IS NOW. RESPECTABLE GRADES AREN'T ENOUGH TO GET INTO THE TOP SCHOOLS!"

Joe and I frowned at each other. "I know that," I began, "but, ah . . ."

"SPEAK UP, BOY!"

"I PLAY BASEBALL!" Joe shouted. "IN THE SPRING! WE'RE BOTH INVOLVED IN THE GREEN ENVIRONMENT CONSERVATION CLUB. AND BESIDES THAT, OUR TIME IS KIND OF TAKEN UP WITH . . . UM . . ."

"EXTRACURRICULAR ACTIVITIES," I put in, "THAT ARE SORT OF . . . WELL . . . OFF THE BOOKS?"

Sleuthing, I tried to tell Principal Gerther telepathically. I wasn't sure how much he knew about our continuing detective work or how he felt about it, so I didn't want to bring it up before he did.

But he was waving his hand dismissively. "THOSE AREN'T ENOUGH," he said.

Suddenly I remembered something that made me sort of righteously indignant. Somehow this led to me raising my hand.

"YES?" Gerther asked, looking a tad annoyed.

"I JOINED THE B-SHARPS A CAPPELLA GROUP!" I shouted defensively. "AND WE WERE JUST

GOING TO HAVE OUR FIRST CONCERT WHEN I GOT CALLED OUT TO COME HERE!"

Principal Gerther looked at me like he smelled something bad. "A CAPPELLA?" he yelled. "THOSE FANCY BOYS IN CARDIGANS WHO SING THE FOUR SEASONS SONGS? NO." He looked down at a piece of paper on his desk and shoved it across to us. "I'M TALKING ABOUT REAL EXTRACURRICULAR ACTIVITIES, BOYS. I'VE TAKEN THE LIBERTY OF SIGNING YOU BOTH UP FOR THE VARSITY BASKETBALL TEAM."

Wha . . . ? I glanced at Joe. *Is he serious?*

Joe looked as startled as I felt. "UM," he said, looking down at the paper, which looked like a practice schedule. The first practice was this afternoon. "THANK YOU? BUT DON'T YOU HAVE TO TRY OUT FOR BASKETBALL? ISN'T THEIR SEASON, LIKE, NEARLY OVER? AND I HAVE PLANS THIS AFTERNOON, WITH MY GIRLFRIEND."

That's when I remembered, the basketball team was actually doing really well this season. According to the morning announcements, they were only two games away from being regional champions, and then they would go to the state championships.

Great, I thought. *So Joe and I will be diving right into the fire.*

Gerther shook his head dismissively. "NORMALLY

YOU WOULD HAVE TO TRY OUT, BUT I'VE MADE AN ARRANGEMENT WITH COACH PEROTTA," he said. "YOU BOYS JUST SHOW UP AT PRACTICE TODAY. I'M SORRY, JOE, BUT YOU CAN SEE YOUR GIRLFRIEND SOME OTHER TIME. I KNOW, JOE, THAT YOU'RE A TALENTED ATHLETE. AND FRANK . . ." He paused and turned to look at me. "I'M SURE YOU WILL CATCH ON."

Yup, greeeeeeeat.

"WHAT ABOUT THE B-SHARPS?" I demanded. *What about my dream?* I thought.

Principal Gerther shrugged. "IF YOU CAN HANDLE BOTH, FINE," he said. "BUT IF NOT, BASKETBALL COMES FIRST. I INSIST."

I pulled my mouth into a tight line, biting back any argument. I knew Principal Gerther. I knew he wasn't going to change his mind. Joe shot me a sympathetic look.

Principal Gerther settled back in his chair. "IF WE UNDERSTAND ONE ANOTHER," he said, "YOU BOYS CAN LEAVE. I BELIEVE IT'S YOUR LUNCHTIME. GO ON AND HEAD TO THE CAFETERIA."

I looked behind us at the clock over the doorway. Gerther was right—the assembly would have ended five minutes earlier. My chance at stardom had been dashed. I would have to bury my disappointment in a turkey sandwich.

"AH, OKAY," said Joe, standing slowly, like he expected Gerther to explain more at any moment. "THANK YOU?"

"YOU'RE WELCOME," barked Principal Gerther, gathering up the loose files on his desk. It was clear the meeting was over.

"This is just freakin' weird," Joe muttered, poking his plastic fork into a row of peas. "I'm really sorry, Marianne."

Joe's girlfriend of two weeks, Marianne Sugarman, shrugged and took a sip of coconut water. Marianne was New Agey and a little ethereal, and I honestly had no idea what she and Joe had in common. She was nice, though.

"It's okay," she said in her melodic voice. "I wish we could hang out, but I get it. It's not like you can say no to Principal Gerther."

"I just don't get why he needs us to play *basketball*," Joe muttered, suddenly squishing a pile of peas under the flat side of his fork.

I knew he was upset then. Joe is protective of his peas.

"Maybe it's just what he said," Marianne suggested with a shrug. "He's worried about your transcripts and wants you to have a better shot with colleges. That's nice of him, right?"

Joe shot me a look that said, *There is no way Principal Gerther would do something nice for us, and we both know it.*

"There has to be *some* reason behind it," I said mildly. "And I guess we'll find out soon enough."

Did you LOVE reading this book?

Visit the Whyville...

Where you can:

- ⬡ Discover great books!
- ⬡ Meet new friends!
- ⬡ Read exclusive sneak peeks and more!

Log on to visit now!
bookhive.whyville.net